BLIND-EYE LOVE

A Young Girl's Abusive Childhood Becomes a Life of Optimism

JP GUGGIA

Library of Congress Control Number: 2025916258

Paperback ISBN: 978-1-966283-97-3
Hardcover ISBN: 978-1-966283-98-0

1. Main category—Literature & Fiction › Literary Fiction › Sagas
2. Other category—Literature & Fiction › Historical Fiction › Women's Fiction
3. Other category—Literature & Fiction › Genre Fiction › Family Life › General

Published by: American Real Publishing
Roger L. Brooks, Publisher
roger@americanrealpublishing.com
americanrealpublishing.com

TABLE OF CONTENTS

Out of suffering have emerged the strongest souls; the most massive characters are seared with scars.

—Khalil Gibran

PROLOGUE

MAKING A COLLECTIVE DIFFERENCE

MANKIND HAS COME A LONG way over the centuries, each era with its own contributions of discovery beyond past generations' perceptions. Realizing we could use Earth's gifts to build and create things, we came up with bigger and better ideas to elevate our lives, with each of those centuries having its individual traumas while society tried to achieve the expansion of human knowledge and capabilities. While these times of achievement have been influenced by the compassionate need to help our world, it's also true that power, money, and ego have been driving factors. What hasn't changed over time is the human need to be relevant, noticed, and in charge. Those needs are met in whatever way each person can manifest them, often with a mindset that has no boundaries for achieving those wants. The goals themselves can cause mental and/or physical abuse to other human beings and cultures. It's too often a belief that the "means justify the end" no matter the cost, human or otherwise.

Let's bring this idea of *justifying the means* into our everyday lives, applying the concept to types of discipline at home or in the workplace. Many of us need boundaries that keep us focused on whatever is expected of us. We respond to being told the right and wrong way to act, to work, to be, forming our personalities in adolescence. Children especially don't have the capacity to understand if what they're told is reality or not. They innately trust their superiors that this must be the right way to be or think. After all, why would they lie to us? Why would they not have our best interest in mind? They tell us they love us, so this must be the right way to act and live.

When you think about the person giving direction in someone else's life, in reality, no one can know what that someone is like until they live with them, or work in their environment, seeing how they react in certain circumstances. What happens in many cases is that the person the outside world sees is nothing like the true person inside. We see how they respond to us and determine that to be the reality of who they are. Interacting with someone else's parent during everyday life, we might think, *She's so sweet!* Or we might say, "Now, there's a great dad." Again, all we see is an outside facade that may or may not represent the true mindset of that person. For many, the way they are perceived is the most important thing. *If they think I'm a good person, then I am.* A person's demeanor and physical appearance have nothing to do with who they are. It's just a visually based assumption that has no bearing on who the actual person is behind that facade, a facade that might be hiding "the end justifies the means" type of person who inflicts abusive pain (mental or physical) to get the results they want with whomever it is they are trying to control.

Applying these ideas explains how the characters in this story became who they were after decades of certain experiences. The story represents a generational Swiss Italian farming family beginning in the 1920s and progressing into today's world. They experienced the Great Depression that started in 1929 with the crash of the stock market, then the horrors of World War II just a few years later. This was a hardworking family that immigrated from Switzerland to the United States, ending up in California where the land was fertile and the weather perfect for growing crops. Opportunities for success seemed within reach. It was a time when people had explicit trust in others, naturally assuming they had more knowledge than you ever could, especially with anyone who had more education than country schooling.

The book's focus is a young girl, Meadow, who suffered under her Aunt Betty's strong will. After circumstances prevailed, the girl's parents, Virginia and George, gave up their baby Meadow to her grandparents, Pete and Jamie. Betty jumped in to help with parenting, to lead the girl on the "right path" by any means possible, while the grandparents looked on. They felt her way of discipline might be too severe yet accepted Betty's way as truth. They were simple people who didn't understand behavior but knew they needed help raising Meadow. Loving them all, they trusted Betty's insight because she was out in the world, had a good job, and had received more education than they had, therefore she must be more intelligent. Not truly knowing what was going on, the extended family and the outside world thought, *The aunt knows what's best. After all, she's pretty and is happy all the time. She's a hard worker and is so good with people. Everyone loves her. And the little girl's mom is just trouble—always has been, always will be. Where would she be without the grandparents and the aunt? Hurt, lonely, or…even dead?*

This is a narrative of mental and physical mistreatment that would be described in today's world as abuse. The word *abuse* has a few meanings:

4.) Misusing the power you have over a situation

5.) Improper use of something (like alcohol)

6.) Treating someone with cruelty or violence on a regular basis

This story is about the third description, revealing abuse that was hidden within the walls of a family dynamic while the outside world was not aware. The victim was aware but didn't *really* know. Typically, the victim of this type of abuse is not able to understand this isn't how things should be, especially if the abuse is from a parental figure they're taught to respect. The rest of the family might say, "No one can know about this," or "It's our family and our business." Fear of letting the outside world know what is truly happening in their (seemingly) idyllic family is a big part of why this kind of mistreatment is so detrimental and continues with no end in sight. Without intervention, a continuous cycle of abuse can move forward through generations because victims are taught the abuse is normal.

Some might say this story of control through verbal and physical harm was necessary out of love and the responsibility of teaching respect. Well-meaning people might think, *If she doesn't do it, no one will. We don't want her turning out like her parents.* These words resonate with people, especially those who assume discipline is what it takes to become a productive person in society. Follow the rules and you will be a good, well-liked person. We do need to follow rules in life, with boundaries being created for our own safety and that of others, so everyone can meet their needs and desires without infringing on anyone else's. Rules are the boundaries of interdependence that is needed for mutual support and cooperation in relationships of every kind within society. But when those rules are used to control, demanding dependency and obedience for power, money, or ego, those ends do not justify the means.

Taken from real life, I've changed the names in this tale. As a storyteller, it's my job to share the facts I've researched while keeping the story interesting for you. As most of the principals are no longer with us for reference, it was necessary to embellish some facts so the impact of the family's journey could be revealed and truly felt, to understand how important sharing these traumas are for awareness. My hope is that you will become more knowledgeable about these complicated situations through acknowledging their existence. The long-term effects of this abuse have devastating consequences, including bulimia, depression, anxiety disorders, PTSD, and can ultimately end in suicide. Fortunately, there are survivors who can rise above this, learning how to put shame and hate in a place that doesn't guide their lives into ruin but instead gives them strength to have productive, rewarding futures. They are the ones who break the chain of abusive behavior, continually striving to understand why this happened while forging ahead in creating a new future free of the bonds of generational trauma.

This tragedy affects as many as 43 percent of boys and girls in their adolescent years. For the record, this is *not* a finger pointing expose to place blame, by any means. Creating awareness is the goal, so we can work toward supporting these victims in confronting the demons constantly haunting them by removing the stigma of shame. Let them know they can announce to the world, "I won't let the past trauma rule me. I can and will overcome that part of my life!" My hope is that they will have understanding and support from today's society to help them recover from the generational mistreatment of their past. While the memories will never go away, forgiving is the key to healing—forgiving the abuser…and *ourselves.*

1

FAMILIAL BEGINNINGS

I N THE LATTER PART OF the 1800s, Switzerland had become overpopulated, with limited job opportunities resulting in widespread poverty. With so much mountainous terrain, farmland became scarce for the growing number of farming families. The government encouraged people to immigrate to other areas of the world to reduce the population pressure, with travel agencies placing ads regularly in Swiss newspapers offering organized crossings of the Atlantic. These soon-to-be immigrants were given 400 Swiss francs, or six months' wages, as incentive to make the ocean voyage to relocate to another country. The United States was a refuge for many of these immigrants, beckoning them to come with promises of a solid future. California was especially inviting as a larger state with miles of coastal land that had median temperatures year-round as well as beautiful meadows of fertile land to grow crops. The land was affordable for these Swiss farmers to purchase and start new lives. Two families especially enjoyed these world gifts, building dairies, houses, and farming the land to become prosperous while providing wonderful lives for their families.

Born in the early part of the twentieth century in California, Pete and Janie came from two of these Swiss Italian families who had migrated from the Italian-speaking cantons of southern Switzerland. They grew up primarily working on their family ranches, receiving some schooling secondarily. Being second generation Swiss Italian, they came up with deep roots of a strong work ethic and respect for the Coastal California countryside they grew up in.

Pete was the oldest in his family. Having asthma as a young boy and into adulthood, he was physically weaker than his other siblings. This prompted his mom, Edie, and the family to protect him, each in their own ways to keep him healthy and taken care of. When he would find his life partner, she needed to be strong, caring, and understanding that the ailment would affect Pete in different ways throughout his life. This was exactly the type of person Janie was.

Pete and Janie's meeting was purely by chance. He was responsible for taking the horse-driven wagon from the ranch into town, to pick up supplies for the dairy and the family every few weeks. Automobiles were becoming the popular mode of transportation, yet many farmers either couldn't afford them or wanted to rely on their old standby of horse and wagon. Pete loved doing this, especially since it was one of the few times things were quiet and serene. Being the oldest of six children, their house could be a chaotic mess. Lots of love for sure but filled with different personalities that sometimes collided with explosive conversation, even a physical altercation here and there. Nothing too bad, but enough for a quiet person like Pete to end up needing some space.

The ride on the dirt road into town was about forty-five minutes from the ranch, which gave Pete time to enjoy the beautiful coastal countryside. It had been a rainy winter, with the spring fields filled with greenery, crops, and a few early spring flowers like lovely blue lupines and stunning orange poppies. He relished these trips to town with the sun shining down and a slight breeze blowing through his hair. He often spent the time pondering the world and where he fit in it. Getting older, he needed to decide where his personal journey would take him. Would he stay at the ranch and keep working at the dairy and in the fields, being a bachelor all his life? Or would he strike out on his own, find a life partner to love and enjoy life with? The answer came much quicker than he ever imagined.

As he was arriving in town, Pete casually looked over and noticed a young girl, smiling, with auburn hair, pink cheeks, and twinkling eyes. The girl exuded happiness and strength that was a magnet for the man. He thought, *Now, this is someone I should get to know.* As his affliction of asthma had slowed down his social life to the point of almost being nonexistent, his chance of meeting a mate seemed extremely remote. This was an opportunity he could not shy away from, and knew he needed to take action.

With the girl intriguing him, he did something he had never done before: Pete decided to be aggressive and turned the wagon around to the house where this young lady was standing on the porch. This family had moved into town from their ranch after the father had passed, leasing the land to others to farm. Their ranch was two thousand acres of fertile land, as well as a dairy, and the rent received allowed them to live a nice, comfortable life.

Looking out to the street and holding on to the porch pole, the girl (Janie) had a smile from ear to ear. Janie's older sister (Dorothy) and their mother (Adelaide) were sitting on the porch in rocking chairs, enjoying the beautiful spring day. Pete pulled up to the house, climbed out of the wagon, and tied the horses to the hitching post. He sauntered up the stone walkway to the porch, his slow-but-sure unassuming demeanor being attractive to this young woman. Even before he reached the house, Janie knew she wanted him to court her.

As he made his way up to the porch, Pete scanned the girl as if he had ex ray vision, peering into her heart and soul. His eyes told him she was a kind, loving person. He assumed she was about twenty years old. She had the full body type he gravitated to, and he loved her auburn hair. It reminded him of his younger sister, Frances's hair, which he always admired.

As the farming community was small, Pete recognized Adelaide, not remembering exactly where from. He immediately knew the family spoke the same Swiss Italian dialect as his family, so he felt comfortable exchanging conversation in their native language. Pete introduced himself, asked their names, and they all shared a bit of conversation: weather, ranching, a touch of politics. He wanted to show he was well rounded, had some knowledge of the world, with a grasp of conversing intelligently. Adelaide was a smart woman, eyeing him up and down. Immediately she was aware that Janie was smitten with him, unlike other men she had been around. Pete was quiet, composed, and not at all forceful with his personality. These attributes were even more appealing to Janie.

The next week there was a spring dance at the local Grange Hall, the building being on the outskirts of town. These halls were built as a community gathering and meeting place for the National Grange of the Order of Patrons of Husbandry, supporting agriculture education and community service for local farming communities. Helping farmers with things such as healthcare and taxation, this was a trusted place for remote farmers to gather. These seasonal dances were held a few times a year to give the locals a chance to unwind and enjoy themselves. With the beginning of the Great Depression and their quiet lives changing, these dances were always looked forward to and well attended.

Pete quietly asked Adelaide if he could take Janie as his date to the dance, knowing full well he had to get her approval. She asked the directed question "Well, how old *are* you?!" Pete proudly responded, "I'm twenty-five years old," thinking his maturity would be something she'd appreciate. Adelaide was not the most polished woman and blurted out, "My Janie is only seventeen. Aren't you a bit old for her?!" Pete assured her his intentions were only honorable, and that he thought Janie was at least twenty, and he wasn't trying to cause their family trouble. Adelaide knew of his family, that he had five siblings younger than him, realizing his poor mother must have had her hands full raising these children. Farm gossip had it that his father was a bit of a drinker, and the rest of the family had to run the farm most of the time. This softened his age and request, so she gave him the ok. "But," she blurted out, "you must take Dorothy along with you. That is that!" Pete knew she meant business, so he gave his ok. Wanting to be in control of the situation, Adelaide told Pete he could meet them there rather than picking the girls up at the house, trying to keep the date more like a meeting rather than a romantic connection. Agreeing, he wondered what she was up to but shrugged it off as an overprotective mother bird trying to keep her precious little bird in the nest.

The next week quickly rolled around. Meeting outside the Grange Hall, they immediately had a bond, went in and started dancing right away. Pete was shyer than Janie but wanted her to think he was in charge and that he loved to dance. Remarkably, his dancing was good enough for the girl to think he was an experienced dancer. Truth was, once he got back home from his supply trip he practiced for hours with his sister Frances.

She knew all the newest dance moves: Jitterbug, the Lindy Hop, Balboa. Frances was the one in the family with style, always knowing what was going on fashionably in the world. The person in charge of the record player chose the best of the current music to play, lots of swing music from Benny Goodman, jazz and ballads from Ella Fitzgerald and Billie Holiday. They danced the jitterbug and held on close when the slow music came on, having the time of their lives. The exciting happiness the young girl felt was so intoxicating she threw her head back and giggled uncontrollably. Pete loved this and laughed right along with her.

Dorothy watched them the whole time, following strict orders from Adelaide. "You watch them like a hawk," she barked at her daughter. "We don't know what this guy is up to, our money or our girl or both!" After a while Dorothy thought to herself, *Oh boy, this girl is going to be with this man.* This was the start of their lifelong romance. There was no turning back for either of them.

With their relationship beginning, Pete would come to Janie's house and spend a few evenings with the family. Then, because Adelaide knew her daughter was falling in love with the man, she finally invited him over for dinners with everyone. Months of dating led to a more physical relationship, Janie becoming pregnant at her young age. While the age difference did not matter to either of them, Adelaide was upset about the whole situation, blaming Pete as the older man. She fought this relationship tooth and nail to not let Janie marry this man. To Janie, Pete was a catch: he came from a good farming family, was a dapper country-boy and handsome man. Pete wasn't ready for children, but with his good upbringing, he knew marrying Janie was the right thing to do. Did he love her? Who knows. His one hope was that Adelaide would eventually lease him her land to grow crops on and run the dairy, his own business being important to him. And maybe even inherit a portion when she passed.

Adelaide had to let go of her blame and gave the ok for the marriage to happen. She couldn't be sure if her initial suspicions of Pete wanting financial gain from her family's fortune was accurate, or if the man did really love her daughter. This was the end of 1929, and a "shotgun" wedding was frowned upon in most circles, especially the close-knit farming community. Whispers were everywhere. The families ignored them and kept their heads held high. There was a small church wedding, Pete dressing in a vested, brown, pin striped suit, Janie wearing a similar colored skirt, blouse, jacket, and hat, her pregnancy not allowing her the honor of wearing a white wedding gown. As was the style, her bouquet was large, in pink tones, trailing to the floor with flowers attached to ribbons. Their union was created, and their together world began. They would have a life of happiness and challenges, challenges that would test their love and longevity through decades of changes that would take its toll on their journey.

Pete and Janie lived with his family, Pete working in the dairy, while Janie helped with house chores. His family loved him, and (seemingly) her but they felt she got pregnant on purpose to snag him. Maybe she did, or maybe it just happened out of love. Janie was treated more like the hired help than any part of the family. She was a hardworking fighter and would not let them get her down by any means.

A few months later, the new baby was born full term, beautiful and perfect in every way. They named her Elizabeth, after Janie's favorite aunt but immediately called her "Betty" as she was so beautiful like the movie star, Betty Amann. Hollywood was just hours south but seemed like a whole world away. Farm people lived a far different life than the movie world, but they loved the idea of seeing movie stars on-screen. His whole family was excited that Pete was making his way in the world and starting a family, while Adelaide suspiciously watched her daughter's life change before her eyes.

A few years later, another daughter came along, and they named her Virginia after one of Pete's aunts. She had the same pink cheeks and twinkle in her little eyes as Janie, her features being more petite than Betty's. This was now their family of four, with no other children in the future. Janie's body could not carry any more children, so there was no boy to carry on Pete's name and heritage. While Pete accepted this fact, it was always in his mind that a boy would never be there for him to teach, share, and love. As time went on, this chipped away at his core, causing just enough resentment to not fully love his daughters. Pete retreated from their children's discipline, giving Janie the job of raising the girls along with anything else they needed. He was never abusive or outwardly mean to them, just not the doting father so many girls need and want in their lives. This would cause a void in their future they didn't understand, one that would challenge them to find love and respect from other men and situations as their lives moved on.

Pete started to get restless about not having his own farming business. He loved his family but just felt he needed to prove his independence. He finally got up the nerve to talk to Adelaide about buying her ranch, keeping it in the family with him and Janie as the owners. He felt making payments would be the only way he could achieve this, not having any money to even give her as a down payment. Pete tried to convince his mother-in-law that he would work hard to make a profit, that fact hoping to entice Adelaide with his offer. "Are you serious?!" she exclaimed. "You're just a poor dairyman who has no money to offer. I let you marry my daughter because she was pregnant but would never trust you to make payments to me to buy my ranch. Find the money for the whole amount, and I'll think about it." Shocked, he meekly said goodbye and went back to his family's ranch, his dreams on hold till he could figure something else out.

As Adalaide became older and feeble, she asked help from her youngest son, Adolfo, who lived in Southern California. Being shrewd and self-ish, he got Adelaide to sign everything over to him: her property, house, and anything else she possessed. Of course, he told her he would share the inheritance with his siblings, her never thinking otherwise. For some reason, he was her favorite, and the woman trusted him without question, which was so out of character for this shrewd person. Her mind "slip-ping" had to be the reason for letting go of everything. With selling the ranch and everything else, Adolfo bought houses in Southern California as income rentals for himself and his own family. He took Adelaide down to live with him until she passed at the age of sixty-six. This became a huge divide with Janie and her siblings, causing irreputable damage to their relationships, with Pete just shaking his head about the whole situation. *Had she only sold the ranch to me, how life would be different* was his constant thought.

Not being able to buy Adalaide's ranch got Pete and his younger brother, Raymond (who wanted his own business as well), to start looking for property to lease. The two always got along well and had great respect for each other. They could trust each other and were both hard workers in their own respects. Janie was right on board with this plan. Just the idea of their own ranch was exciting for her. They searched and ended up finding a working dairy ranch farther south that they could lease indefinitely. The property was a few hours from his parents' ranch, near a smaller California town, just a couple miles from the Pacific Ocean. There was a huge amount of agricultural land around with a dairy they could work on while growing alfalfa and corn as feed for the herd. They had lived with Pete's family for some years, and it was time to move on with their own lives.

Pete, Janie, and their two girls moved to their "new" house and ranch, hiring working men to help Pete and Raymond with the heavy workload a dairy demands. This was such an honor for these men, to be trusted and given the chance to work hard and make something of their lives on this dairy ranch. Their lives would all be tested over the years, revealing their strengths and fortitude to survive.

2

GOOD TIMES

ONCE THEY MOVED IN AND settled, the dairy and farming got into full working order. Janie ran the household, cooking three meals a day for the family and all the working men. She cleaned, kept the bills paid, grew vegetables and flowers in an area adjacent to the house. If a working man was sick, she filled in on the dairy doing what needed to be done. A stout woman who forged ahead no matter what, she was the force behind making everything work and determined not to give up. She wore a housecoat dress, cotton overhead tie-back apron, black nurse's work shoes, and a corset with nylons. Janie's hair grayed early, her auburn locks fading away, keeping her thick, wavy hair shorter than during her youth. And, oh, those pink cheeks! She could easily have been Mrs. Clause in any performance.

While Janie was the working backbone of the family and a no-nonsense person who would not put up with any shenanigans, she was also caring with a hearty, sweet laugh. She demanded respect from everyone. If you were smart, you'd give her a pleasing phrase to keep her happily on your side. "Thank you, I appreciate all that you do" is something she'd love to hear. At the same time, Pete, Raymond, and the working crew made sure the ranch was run properly. They milked daily, along with planting the crops they used for animal feeding. Then harvest time would come, and everyone was on board to make sure the corn and alfalfa were processed properly.

Daughters Betty and Virginia were taught chores at a young age. They learned how to clean, scrub the floors, peel potatoes, dust, and anything else that needed to be done. They also had to work on the ranch after school. The sisters would shovel cow poop, take pitchforks and separate bales of hay, and put sections of that hay into the cows' feeding troughs. Janie was patient with their learning, but as they got older, her demands became concrete: "Do it the right way or else!"

Betty and Virginia started dressing themselves at an early age, making sure their hands and faces were washed before coming out to breakfast or any meal. When they were of school age, Janie made sure they caught the bus to their country school, with prepared lunches in hand. She was there with open arms when the bus brought them home from school. Then it was on to their daily duties.

The dairy business was their financial mainstay. Milking cows is a tough job, going to work at four a.m., milking the herd, feeding, going back to the house for breakfast, napping, then back for milking the second time at one p.m. till four p.m. It's a continuous cycle that keeps the milk flowing, selling to processing companies like Knudsen who pasteurized and packaged the milk for sale. The Great Depression had begun in 1929 due to overvaluing product on the American Stock Exchange. The market crashed, having a rippling effect across the globe. Millions were out of work for an extended time, with the Red Cross and other charities providing food lines in most cities that fed those without financial resources. While this affected some farmers, Pete and his family seemed to keep things going, milk being a product everyone wanted. While the profit margin was low because of pricing, they were still able to make their payments and handle the business. There were five dairies in the area, all friendly, ready to help each other. It was a true testament of the times, with a shared solidarity necessary for everyone's survival. The Great Depression was on its way to being over, with its remnants engrained in those that experienced this devastating time in our country's evolution.

3

THE RANCH HOUSE

THE RANCH HOUSE SAT BACK from the main road, north of the dusty trail that led to the back section of the barn where the milking was done. The road was lined with tall eucalyptus trees, shielding their house from the Pacific Ocean winds that could be fierce at times. The house had a tall hedge around three sides, protecting the front door (which was rarely used) and porch from view. It was a traditional farmhouse: large kitchen, three bedrooms, and one bathroom. The washroom, with its large sink and a washing machine, was part of the back porch entry that looked out to the bunkhouse. The area between the house and the bunkhouse was trellised and covered with lush grapevines overhead. The back door was the entry of choice for everyone, any time of the day or night.

The kitchen was the center of the household, where eating and business conversations took place. It had a large, rectangular table, with benches on either side to seat twelve people comfortably where three meals a day were served. Janie became an expert at cooking and baking. She was organized and always served meals on time. Using the vegetables she grew and meat from their local butcher, her meals were delicious and always complete with a main portion of meat, some sort of potatoes, and a vegetable. A bit of local homemade wine was served along with a dessert she had created.

The living room had a brick fireplace with a mantel and mirror above. The long couch could seat four people comfortably with two end tables and lamps. The three other chairs offered more seating to listen to the console radio in the corner, and, eventually, a television. One chair was an American Rocker, while the other two were comfortable navy-blue armchairs that welcomed guests to enjoy their company. Raymond's bedroom was off the living room with a double bed, nightstand, cedar chest, and a dresser with a mirror attached. The windows were covered with sheer curtains, keeping things a bit private but also letting the sun light ease in.

To the right of the kitchen (before the living room) was the hall leading to the other two bedrooms and bathroom. The floor heater was smack-dab in the middle of the hall, so you had better wear shoes to walk on its hot surface (*if* the heater was on as Janie was a thrifty lady). The bathroom was at the end of the hall with the traditional porcelain bathtub (separate faucets for hot and cold), a toilet, and a porcelain pedestal sink. Cabinets lined the wall for linens and anything else. The master bedroom was on the right, appointed with simple furnishings, nice warm bedding, and the same sheer curtains. The left bedroom was Betty and Virginia's, with a twin bed for each girl, a night table and lamp in between. The girls shared a dresser and a small closet. Their amount of clothing was minimal, yet always clean, pressed, and cared for.

The bunkhouse was back from the house, about thirty yards. It was not fancy by any means but suitable for the eight working men who helped at the dairy and ranch. Meager in its decor and single-walled construction, it served its purpose for the transient types who filled the employment positions the ranch needed. These men all had rough backgrounds, with lives that hadn't gone the way they thought, many with a deep sadness because of this. Happy to have a job, they also loved the family atmosphere Janie created for them with her wonderful meals and happy smile. During these difficult financial times, these men were grateful to have jobs, working hard, long hours to prove themselves while making money they could start a new life with.

Hard work and saving money were the mode in this family's life. Times were different then, and this family slowly realized there was a need to cope with problems they had no idea how to handle. There was no one to reach out to, no one to help them the way they needed, and too much shame once the future brought what it would. This house was their safe spot, close enough to town, yet far enough away to have a country life, a life they were used to that embraced who they were.

4

DEVILISH FIEND

FROM A NOTICEABLY YOUNG AGE it was evident that something was not quite right with Virginia. She was physically healthy, growing at the proper rate for her various ages. Yet her behavior was constantly sporadic. She would throw tantrums one minute, then the next be giggling uncontrollably, followed with a calm demeanor for a time. Janie thought she was just acting out for attention and let it go at that. As she grew, she became a handful to raise, defiant at every turn. Virginia would balk at any of her duties, eventually giving in, making her bed or whatever chore Janie had instructed her to do. It was always "Why do I have to make my bed? I will just mess it up again tonight!" Then she would run to her room and begin acting as if someone were there in the room with her, carrying on conversations that did not seem to make sense when Janie overheard her. "Must be an imaginary friend she's talking to," Janie would say under her breath. "What else could it be?"

During these times, Janie kept trying to correct Virginia's behavior, thinking a slap here and there would keep her in line. It got to be "Oh, that's just Virginia" and left at that. Weeks of stability would camouflage the undiagnosed bipolar and schizophrenic disorder she suffered from for years. Adding to the problem was that Virginia was just so darn cute with a pixie haircut and those twinkling eyes that complemented her tiny face. When asked a question, those mischievous eyes would squint, her head laying to the left looking at you like, *What the hell are you talking about?!*, then adding a small, narcissistic evil smile with the statement. It seemed at seven years old she could charm anyone, and if you embraced her and gave her attention, she was yours. And so her life continued, her condition's symptoms spread out over time, not allowing others to quite understand her changing personality.

With the working men coming in and out of the house daily for meals, they got to know the girls well. They loved how Virginia was coy yet forward and how Betty was beautiful and demure. Virginia became the favorite with some of these men, even though Betty was more of a natural beauty. Virginia had small, cute features and was more outgoing and friendly, while Betty stayed in the background. She let Virginia take center stage, afraid to go ahead of her younger sister. *Let her look forward,* she thought. *I will be the one they like better*, was her "good girl" mantra for years.

One worker, Leroy, was especially fond of Virginia. He would bring Virginia gifts, boxes of candy, and small, inexpensive jewelry, always chatting with her about this or that. He would give Betty a small trinket so it wouldn't look like he favored Virginia. He lavished Virginia with attention, and the little girl was loving every minute of it, feeling so special.

Not publicly known in the local farming industry, Leroy was the only child from a wealthy family in San Francisco. His father was a hotelier, owning multiple high-end properties. Leroy had graduated from Stanford Business School, with plans to eventually step in to run the family business. But his heart wanted to be with the earth's soil. Leroy loved the outside nature of the farming industry and decided to travel south to physically work on a farm, getting to know the ins and outs from the ground up. He was not corporate material by any means, and wanting to go on some wild search "to find himself" was frowned on by his family. They argued with him for days about his decision, knowing this would have been the perfect time for Leroy to be part of the family legacy. Finally, they just let him go to experience the world he thought he wanted to live in.

Leroy took the train and ended up at the coastal village a couple miles from Pete, Janie, and Raymond's ranch. He walked east on the main road till he came to their ranch, which was the first one heading east. He was hired on the spot, and Leroy was now in the hands of Pete and Raymond to train him and show him the hard life of farming that can net you great rewards as well. He kept his background to himself not wanting them to think he was just a rich kid playing a game. Leroy made up some story about being from Northern California, born to a family that worked in service for the wealthy folk in the area. He knew that would endear him to this family even more, being of a more "common" life circumstance.

Janie and Pete enjoyed Leroy's company, as well as others on their working men team. Leroy was humorous, polite, complimentary—three traits that were important to them. He was five-foot-ten, with dark curly hair, and naturally muscular. Handsome compared to the other workers, he could charm anyone with a wink and a smile. Janie and Pete were captivated by Leroy's charming nature…so much so that the couple invited him to listen to evening radio shows in their living room. During these shows, many times Pete and Janie would fall asleep on the couch and chair, both laying back and snoring, their heads tilted with their bodies slouching in dreamland. Betty and Virginia would already be tucked away safe and sound in their beds, fast asleep, wearing their cotton fleece nightgowns, long sleeved with frilly fabric around their necks and wrists. Bought at the local JCPenney store, these nightgowns kept the girls warm and comfy in a house that could be cold from the coastal fog that frequently floated in.

One night, Leroy was invited to listen to the radio with Pete and Janie. When the girls' parents had fallen asleep, Leroy thought, *This is my chance to be close to her.* He made sure the parents were asleep, then slowly got up from the rocking chair that faced the radio and began quietly walking down the hall to the girls' bedroom. Taking slow, deliberate steps, he made sure he did not step on the heater floor vent as to make any extra noise. While Betty was deeply asleep, Virginia was still awake. Sometimes her mind would not let her stop thinking about things, seeing pictures of everyday life flashing in her brain as if they were horses on a merry go round going faster and faster.

Leroy quietly opened the bedroom door, walked over to Virginia's bed, and carefully lifted her out. While she could feel his presence approaching, she pretended to be asleep, thinking that this was Leroy being nice to her. *He likes me best!* she thought. *How special am I!* They moved slowly to the bathroom next door, Leroy closing the door in a way so no one would hear. His heart was racing, yet Virginia's was quite calm. He set her down on her feet, whispering to her, "Don't be afraid. I would never hurt you." Leroy lifted her nightgown, pulled down her cloth panties, then gently started to fondle Virginia's young body. He kissed her all over, not aggressively, nor wanting to scare her—only to honor her as his "sweet Virgie."

No matter how deranged this sexual encounter was, his mind rationalized it as an act of his true love for Virginia. He did not ask to be touched and was extremely gentle. The little girl couldn't quite figure out what was going on, not screaming or making a sound. It was one of those clear, coastal evenings, the full moon casting a soft glow of light through the small lace embellished window onto this perverse scene. Virginia could see his face clearly. Leroy was on his knees in front of her with eyes closed, breathing heavily, his hot breath billowing in and out of his mouth. Expressionless, she stood there frozen, accepting his "affection." *Does he still love me?* she thought. *Is this how love is supposed to be?* With Virgina's confusion, it was fortunate this lasted just a few moments. Leroy gently pulled up her panties, lowering her nightgown down. He lifted Virginia back up, and they quietly left the bathroom. He gently laid her on the bed so his *princess* could sleep. He kissed her forehead, whispering, "Sleep well, my lovely girl."

He then crept back to the living room where the radio was still on, some news show sharing whatever was important that day, while Janie and Pete floated in their dreams. The Early American rocker welcomed him, unaware of the damage he had just done. Virginia drifted off to sleep feeling conflicted as a child would be not understanding Leroy's way of showing he loved her. A dream entered her sleep, one about the devil she had learned about at the Catholic church. This devil was Leroy, his fiery face and horned head being inches away from her face, with his hot, stinky breath smothering her. Virginia suddenly woke up, shaking and sitting upright. "Leroy must be the devil," she whispered softly. "I need him to go away!"

She did not dare mention this to anyone. Virginia knew her family would blame her for being "too" friendly to that Leroy devil, letting him fool her into thinking that he loved her. As usual, she would have gotten in trouble, being told she was too friendly with the men and caused this herself. *Better to keep quiet and figure something out.* While Virginia's lack of fatherly affection kept her searching for the masculine love and acceptance she wanted badly, this love from Devil Leroy was not what she needed.

The next day, the girls were playing in the ranch tool shed, blowing on spider webs, rummaging through all the tools and collected goodies that ended up in the old wooden structure. The afternoon sun was sneaking through a loose board on the shed's wall that focused on something that caught Virginia's eye: a rusty hammer, oversized, meant for larger nails. "I love this, Betty," Virginia said in that sweet voice she could conjure up when she needed to. Betty turned, saying, "Virginia, put that down. It's dangerous!" Because she was the older sister, Betty thought she could oversee Virginia, which her sister would never allow. "Shut up," Virginia said, her usual response. "I'm taking it as a gift."

That night, after Janie got the girls into their beds and kissed them goodnight, Janie, Pete, and Leroy were listening to their favorite musical radio performance, *The Fred Waring Show*. The beautiful orchestra music and talented singers took them away from their everyday work lives into another realm beyond their little farm in the country. Raymond was already in bed fast asleep in the bedroom right off the living room. He bedded down early knowing he needed proper rest to keep those workers in line the next day.

The house was quiet otherwise, the girls seemingly fast asleep. Virginia had put her newfound gift under the bed for safekeeping. She whispered to Betty, "Are you asleep?" There was no answer from Betty, which was exactly what she hoped. Slowly getting up and out of bed, Virginia put her hand under the bed, grabbed the tool, and headed for the living room. She whispered "I'm taking care of that devil. He will not bother me again." Her voice was confident and determined, with not one bit of fear about what she had in store for Leroy.

Soon Pete and Janie drifted off to sleep, their snoring loud enough to be heard but not to stop Leroy from humming along to the music blaring on the radio. He thought about paying his Sweet Virgie a visit. Unfortunately for him, the thought came too late. Virginia quietly crept up the hallway, peering around the corner of the wall to make sure her parents were asleep. Hearing the loud snoring she knew this was her chance to sneak up behind Leroy. The back of Leroy's rocking chair faced the living room entry, his head rising above the tied-on cushion of the comfortable chair. Virginia snuck up behind him, lifted the heavy tool with her small arms and both hands, and smashed Leroy on the back of the head as hard as she could.

"Take that you devil!" she screamed as the tool gashed his skin, blood shooting out from the wound.

"What the *fuck*?!" Leroy yelled at the top of his lungs, grabbing the back of his head, blood spilling onto the back of the chair and the floor.

The screams jolted Pete and Janie out of their dreamy sleeps, and they, too, screamed at what they saw.

Virginia quickly dropped the bloody tool, not noticing Leroy's blood had splattered all over her nightgown. She ran to her room and burrowed under her bed blankets, staining her sheets with the blood as well. While the girl was scared, she was confident she had taken care of that devil. "He won't bother me again," she said softly. The little girl was proud of herself for taking control of the situation and did not care one bit if he died or was scarred for life.

Betty woke up, super confused. "What's going on, Virginia?!" she yelled out.

Viginia only replied, "Be quiet!"

Hearing all the commotion, she rushed to the living room. She was appalled and scared of what she saw, this poor man bleeding and moaning. Her mind immediately knew that her sister had done one more thing for attention. *Darn that Virginia…always causing trouble!*

Janie and Pete jumped up from the couch, Janie running to get towels from the bathroom, the same room Leroy had molested Virginia in the night before. She got back to the living room with the towels, her body shaking from the chaos. The woman knew she had to get this man's wound cleaned to see the damage Virginia had done. "I'll take care of you, Leroy… Sorry for this happening!" she said this with such urgency, her heart pounding and breathing labored as if she had just run from the barn.

"It's ok, Janie. I know she did not mean it." Leroy knew damn well why this happened. He did not worry or have remorse. If necessary, he knew he'd be protected by his wealthy family that would throw money at these hardworking people.

Janie cleaned his wound, getting the area behind the rocker cleaned up as well. Their rugs might be old, but she was not going to let them get stained by this tragedy. Pete just stood there in shock. It was as if all this was going in slow motion, not seeming real. Janie needed his help, he shook it off and got into action. Realizing Leroy would need stitches, the decision was quickly made for Pete to drive Leroy to the hospital. An ambulance would take way too long to get out to their country ranch.

Raymond was in a deep sleep when the commotion woke him up. Even though his bedroom was right off the living room, he rarely woke during the night until it was time to get his crew going, usually getting up at three a.m. He jumped up, put on his jeans, and came out just as Pete was taking Leroy to his truck. Raymond followed them, waiting till they got to the truck to find out what had happened to one of his working men. Pete quickly filled him in with the sordid details.

Raymond was in total disbelief, his anger building, ready to take it out on somebody for this tragedy that had just occurred. Leroy had always been one of his top guys, never any trouble and always a hard worker. "Pete, why would our little Virginia do such a crazy thing to Leroy?!" he blurted out.

Pete was calmly in disbelief about the whole situation as well, his voice trembling yet calm.

"I don't know, but I sure as hell am going to find out!" Then Raymond yelled out to Leroy, "Get taken care of. I need you at work!"

Leroy knew he needed to respond like a wounded character in a play, innocent, yet forgiving of Virginia. "I'll be fine, don't worry, Raymond," he said like a mournfully damaged victim.

Pete jumped in the pickup and drove the country road to the hospital a few miles away into town.

He stayed with Leroy until he was examined and stitched up, the wound not being nearly as bad as all the blood led everyone to believe. Had an adult used the tool on Leroy's head, he probably wouldn't be alive. The man was lucky his attacker was small and petite, which is why he molested her in the first place. The doctor decided Leroy should stay in the hospital overnight in case there was a concussion from the accident. The man fought it, but Pete insisted as well, not wanting any problems from this incident.

Pete headed back to the ranch in his trusted pickup truck. Unlike the clear previous night, this evening was dark and foggy, with no moon shining to light up the country roads. Pete was still in disbelief this all happened. *Why would Virginia do this? Was it a dream? And if it wasn't a dream, what did Leroy do to the little girl to make her so mad she wanted to hurt him?* These were questions this simple man could not find answers to. He had to dismiss the situation and just chalk it up to one of "those" things. The cows needed milking soon, so he needed to get back to bed and get some rest. "If only I had a boy to raise," he murmured. "None of this would have happened."

After all the commotion, Janie needed a shot of whiskey to calm her nerves. She sat for a minute, trying to grasp this situation, with no answers as to why this would happen. Realizing she needed to change Virginia's sheets and nightgown and then clean the girl up, she went to the girls' room. While she was changing Virginia's nightgown, Janie asked, "Why would you do such a thing, Virgina? And where did that tool come from?!" The girl confidently replied, "I had a scary dream that Leroy was the devil and I had to get rid of him so we all could be safe. I was just trying to help, Mama."

"She took the tool from the tool shed," Betty proudly announced.

Virginia gave her sister the most severe look of disdain, claiming, "I just thought the hammer might be something to have in the house so I could protect us all," making it sound like her only goal was to help her family.

Janie just shook her head. "Please don't do anything like this again. Good working men are hard to come by, and we need Leroy to help us at the ranch."

"I promise, Mama," that coy twinkle in her eyes saying just the opposite. Virginia could not let on how ecstatic she was that she took care of that devil and didn't care if he lived or died. "I got you, you creepy devil" was the mantra going through her little brain. She was proud that she defended her family. No shame in that!

Janie tucked the girls in, kissed them goodnight, and went back to the living room to view "the scene of the crime" one more time.

The hammer was still lying on the floor, so she grabbed it and threw it into the outside garbage can. Janie's mind shifted to getting ready for the following workday. Her goal was to keep this ranch going with her end of the workload, no matter what. Pete finally returned from the hospital and updated Janie and Raymond. Janie revealed Virginia's reason for creating this dangerous chaos. The men were in disbelief, both shaking their heads in unison. They all headed to their respective beds as the morning would soon be here. Getting the work done was the most important thing to these people. It gave them purpose and showed that they were quality people. The rest would take care of itself.

The family fabricated some excuse about this being a farm accident, not placing any blame on Virginia…or Leroy, for that matter. Naturally, Leroy kept quiet about everything and soon moved on to another ranch. He finally decided to go back to his family, traveling to the Bay Area by train. They were excited for their boy to return. He had followed his dream, telling them he realized that farm life wasn't for him. His fear of being found out about his molestation got him thinking he better get to the safety of his family. Preparing to help run the family business, Leroy began having reoccurring, severe headaches that would debilitate him to the point of only staying in bed. As there was no way to detect brain tumors in the 1930s, doctors assumed he had some type of brain disease with no cure available. He passed away a year later, alongside his family who only knew their son as a smart, handsome, and kind man who followed his heart. They had no idea about the "Virgie" incident, or that the head wound he got during the farm accident (he claimed happened) in the milking barn had anything to do with his death.

This whole situation was dismissed, being pushed aside by the total ranch family. No one discussed the unusual happenings or tried to figure out why this really happened. There was no time to bother with this now that everything had calmed down. Leroy had moved on, Virginia was her usual obstinate self, and everyone's primary job was to keep this ranch profitable, keeping food on the table and the lights on. "Our work never stops on this ranch," Janie would say. "We don't have time for any non-sense, so let's get things done!"

Beneath this little girl's surface was a force brewing that grew as time went on. The psychological damage of Leroy's devil forced Virginia to start mentally protecting herself—a protection, along with continued defi-ance, that was innate to the girl at an early age but now even more pro-nounced because of the sexual assault. She had gotten rid of that evil, yet the extreme trauma from the experience was pushed further back in her psyche, eventually coming to the surface in ways few would understand. Especially with not understanding the true nature of the girl's mental ill-ness, undiagnosed and left to guide her life of defiance and confusion.

5

IRISH EVIL

T HE GREAT DEPRESSION FINALLY ENDED in 1939, but our world would not be at peace. World War II started in September of that year, with German Nazis invading Poland, a country that had been guaranteed miliary support from Great Britain and France. These countries' commitment to Poland prompted the declaration of war on Germany two days later. With Adolf Hitler and his millions of Germans actively supporting the regime, Germany and World War II was ravaging Europe. Paris and many other cities became occupied by the Nazi's, changing their population's way of life for this brief period. Like many Germans, Hitler became obsessed with the extermination of the Jewish population. Some say this hatred came from situations he experienced at a young age, but there is no concrete proof of why these feelings developed. This created one of the most despicable times in our modern world, creating havoc and the ruining of millions of lives within just a few years. Japan became an ally of Germany, setting their sights on bombing Hawaii's Pearl Harbor in 1941. This provoked President Roosevelt to sign an executive order authorizing the military to send Japanese families living on the WestCcoast of the United States to internment camps more inland. The political consensus was that *those people* could be spies for the Japanese government, creating unnecessary national panic as well as extreme Japanese racial hate. Many Japanese families had migrated to the coastal communities of California over the years, having come to this country from Japan to work on farms as experienced farm laborers, most of them becoming tenant farmers and eventually wealthy landowners.

Some of these families had settled in Pete and Janie's farm area. The land was fertile, and with the medium temperatures year-round, these seasoned farmers made valuable contributions to the local farming community. When the internment situation was happening, Pete and Janie decided to help one of the Japanese families, hiding them in their cellar, providing them food, water, and whatever else they needed for the two years of the internment law. While this was a time of turmoil and grief affecting millions of people in the world, Pete, Janie, Raymond, and the girls needed to continue with their country lives, keeping the family prosperous while giving work to as many men as the farm needed. With the drafting law of men for the military in effect, the farmers were fortunate to be exempt from this law. These ranch families were crucial in providing food and milk goods for the war effort, as well as all the people countryside who cheered on our military.

By 1942, Nazi Germany had a strong hold on most of Europe and the war was in full military motion. While this affected the world, the ranch seemed somewhat isolated from these wicked happenings. Life went on, work needed to be done, girls had to be raised as best they could.

Betty was now twelve, with her body beginning its physically mature transition. Her menstrual cycle had begun, along with breast development and her body's natural curves. She was becoming an attractive woman, coming out of her shell of standing in the back of the crowd, being friendly to everyone with her nice smile. As discussion about a girl's natural body functions were rarely shared during this time, both she and Virginia had to figure some things out on their own. While Betty accepted what was going on with her body, she would shyly ask Janie "Why is this happening to me, Mama?" Janie's response was direct and clear: "That's just how it is when you're a woman. You'll bleed every month and need to wear something to keep the blood from running down your leg." That's as much as Janie knew, generations just accepting these facts, while not truly understanding the "why" of it all. Betty did what she was told and went about her life.

It was spring, and the first alfalfa harvest was going on, the second completed in the summer. All the workers were in the fields, bailing hay with their automatic baler and throwing the bales on the flatbed trailer. They had advanced to quality motor-driven trucks, and farm life was much easier with these machines. Pete always drove the truck, with Raymond working the men to get the job done. With Pete's asthma, Raymond was the more physical part of their work team and ruled the workers with an iron fist. They respected him and knew better than to fall behind in their work.

The left-over hay bales from the previous harvest were kept in one part of the dairy, away from the main milking stalls. These were older stalls where cows were kept if they needed extra care or were ready to "drop their calf," the term used for giving birth to their newborn. Hay still needed to be put in the troughs, which was one of the girls' chores. They would take hay from the loose bales that were across from the feeding area with a pitchfork, placing it into a wheelbarrow, pushing the wheelbarrow over to the trough, then unloading the loose hay into the trough. This part of the barn was a catch all for old tools that were obsolete or so rusted out their lifespan was over and done. These were tossed in piles at one end of the trough area, while the other areas were less cluttered. The one common thing was the familiar aroma of cow poop that tended to linger until it would be cleaned up by the men after the hay bailing was finished. This day, Virginia was sick, so Betty was doing the chore by herself after school.

"That darn Virginia, always making things up so she doesn't have to work," Betty said out loud. "Of course, I'm here to take up the slack." Betty never used cuss words like Virginia. She was too proper for that kind of language.

"Aye, lassie, and I'm glad ya are," a voice from behind said, in a strong Irish brogue.

Startled, she turned around and saw Patrick, one of the working men. He was Irish, a small man, with red hair parted in the middle, and missing a few teeth. He wasn't the most attractive person but was always cordial and a good worker. His family immigrated to New York from Ireland after World War I, his father and uncle starting a butcher shop from their work experiences in their homeland. Patrick's father's whiskey drinking was always a problem. The man would get drunk, beat his wife and children, getting them to do whatever he wanted, no one being immune to anything the man desired.

After the Great Depression started and their butcher shop closed for lack of business, both families headed to California where they heard you could buy cheap land and start farming. His uncle had saved some money and bought land, starting a farming business in the coastal area where Pete, Raymond, and Janie had their ranch. Both Irish families worked the fields, but Patick's father just couldn't give up the drink, and died while he was plowing a field, his liver shot from his alcohol abuse. Patick followed in his father's footsteps and was a whiskey drinker like him. His uncle finally had to send him away, yelling, "Aye, lad, take your Irish Goodbye and learn ya own life." Raymond knew the family and offered Patrick a job at their ranch when he saw him walking the roads looking for work. They needed extra help, so he figured he may as well give him a chance. Unfortunately, Raymond wasn't aware of the generational evil possessing Patrick from the years of adolescent beating and his father's raping.

Startled from Patrick's voice, Betty questioned, "Oh, Patrick! Why aren't you out in the field?" He replied, "Aye, Lassie, I snuck away to make sure ye wer doin' ye job right. With yer sister sick, I thought ye might need some help." His eyes were wide open when he was talking to her, coming closer inch by inch, making her uncomfortable. His alcohol breath was so rancid it almost knocked her out. Patrick had been eyeing Betty for some time, attracted to her natural beauty and sweet smile, becoming obsessed with her as Leroy was with Virginia.

Patrick made his way right up to Betty, not pausing for a moment. He suddenly grabbed her, gently pulling her over to the side where the loose hay made a soft pile. He was not rough, just forceful with his motions, laying her down on the bed of hay. "This won't take long," he whispered. "I just need ye to let me take care o' myself."

Betty had changed from her school clothes into her work overalls, with an old, long-sleeved blouse underneath. He slowly unbuttoned the straps of the overalls, pulling them down to her ankles, her blouse in place, then removing her panties down to her scrunched overalls. She closed her eyes, not understanding what was happening. Betty was taught to do as her elders told her, whatever they asked. In no way would she be like that Virginia, always questioning and causing trouble. She was a good girl and knew she needed to do what an adult told her.

Patrick pulled down his pants, showing his Irish adult body, and laid on top of the fearful girl. There was no gentle anything about his actions. Knowing Betty had to be a virgin, Patrick entered her without taking his time, forcing his way in with no regard for her feelings. Her pain was excruciating, but the girl did not let out a whimper. This took only a minute, and once he was finished, he pulled up his pants, then pulled her overalls and panties up, rebuttoning the straps, pulling her upright.

"Thank ye, lil lady," he quietly said. "Let's keep this between us. I wouldn't want ye to get in trouble for not doing yer work, slacking off and taking a break. Bye, lassie… See ye at dinner." He said this nonchalantly, as if nothing happened, that this was just another day's occurrence.

As Patrick turned and walked away, he decided to give the girl a little wink to be that much more obnoxious. The man was not equipped with remorse of any kind, like a serial killer who takes their time dismembering bodies for fun. As he pivoted around, he noticed one strap had become unbuttoned on her overalls. He started back toward Betty, her body frozen in place like an ice statue, riddled with fear. Patrick gently buttoned the strap securely, staring right into the fragile girl's eyes.

The rapist finally walked away. Betty just stared at him. She was in a daze for a few minutes, then went back to work as if nothing had happened. She was in pain but knew she couldn't tell anyone; it was much safer for her to just forget about it and not stir up trouble like her sister. *Was she bad for letting it happen? What did it all mean?* Without the knowledge she needed, it became an experience that was just something to get over. An experience that would not allow her to fully embrace her body or future physical relationships with men. Betty was now mentally damaged, damage that she hid from herself so deep it wasn't allowed to rule her life. It was a pain that would reveal itself in ways no one could imagine, making her control the people closest to her that had no defense mechanism to stop the abusive discipline she enforced later in life.

From this point on, Betty was wary of all the working men. She knew most of them were nice, hardworking men who helped her family so much. She was still friendly, just more reserved than ever around them. Especially Patrick. He would wink at her now and then, her eyes looking through him as if he was invisible. Janie noticed she was not quite the same around the men as before, wondering why, just for a moment. Then she dismissed it as part of her daughter's pre-teen growing up. Janie had way too much to do without conjuring up something that wasn't even there.

Patrick had no remorse whatsoever about his sexual abuse of Betty. It was if he wanted it, it happened, and it was over. Then his time just traveled on. The part of his brain that should have felt this remorse was damaged beyond repair. His father's drunken mistreatment of Patrick and his family had somehow rearranged his brain into a factory of two-dimensional thinking, not processing good or bad the same way most people react to in life situations. He ended up quitting the ranch, drifting to the eastern part of California, where the summers are brutally hot, unlike the coastal summers he had been living in. The foggy days that lasted for weeks were a bad reminder of his young years in Ireland where the weather is wet and cold, so he thought he would give this a try. No ties, no family wanting him around. He was free to do as he pleased.

He got a job working in one of the large apple orchards, hauling picked apples to the barn where they stored the fruit before shipping. One late afternoon, he pulled into the barn and saw the orchard manager's ten-year-old daughter playing, singing "We're Off to See the Wizard" from the famed *The Wizard of Oz* movie she had once seen at the theater. She was running in and out of the rows of crated apples, singing sweetly and enjoying this afternoon time before dinner.

She didn't hear the truck coming in as Patrick had slowed way down after he eyed the little girl. Her name was Ruby, named after the color of the slippers Judy Garland wore in the movie. Her mother adored the book and movie, along with all its characters. He slowly got out of the truck, his eyes intent on the young girl, and walked over to where she was playing. Startled like Betty was, she turned around to see who was there. Patrick pushed the girl to the ground, starting to pull her dress up. His eyes were wide open, his breathing heavy with the scent of booze and rotted teeth. Ruby frantically screamed as loud as she could, unlike Betty, who thought she needed to stay quiet and not draw attention to what was happening to her. This alarmed anyone nearby, especially her father, Jerry, who was working in the adjacent office. Jerry grabbed the pistol he kept in his desk for protection from transients and others who might try to steal from the orchard and ran as fast as he could into the barn. He knew his daughter's scream and that something was terribly wrong. Two other workers ran in after him, ready to help with whatever their boss needed.

Seeing the terrible happenings, Jerry pulled Patrick off the girl, pushed him into an aisle, then shot him right in the chest, yelling, "Take that, you Mick bastard!" at the top of his lungs, killing the man immediately. He never liked or trusted Patrick, so this was a safe way of ending his employment without any backlash. All the other workers were gone for the day, so the two remaining were told to take the body to a far part of the field and bury him deep into the ground. With no relatives or friends, there would be no questions where this guy would be. They obeyed without hesitation, knowing that helping the boss was in their best interest. Jerry pulled Ruby up, hugged her tighter than ever, saying "He won't hurt you anymore. I love you, Ruby!" They slowly walked to their on-site house a few hundred feet away and didn't speak of this again.

The story told to the other employees was that Patrick took off in a drunken rage and no one knew where he went after traveling down that long, dusty trail to the main road. Young Betty was scarred forever, yet (fortunately) the world was now a much safer place without this testosterone driven man's mis-wired brain telling him to satisfy only *his* needs, with no more harm coming to other unsuspecting young girls that were in his demented sights.

6

FRAGMENTED CONTROL

YEARS TRAVELING ON AS THEY do, the family learned, little by little, to handle things that came their way. Pete, Janie, and Raymond kept the ranch going financially, keeping those noses of theirs to that daily grindstone. It was how they were taught to live: the more you work, the better you are. Betty and Virginia were now young ladies in high school living their lives, not knowing what the future would bring. Their childhoods now behind them, with those abhorrent memories tucked deeply away where no one could find them, they were hopeful to find a man and live happy lives. This was barely post–World War II, a time when our country was beginning to prosper after the horrors of that war, the Holocaust and the Nazi invasions being devastating to much of the world. Reeling from these horrors, it was a time when hope was a word that rang true, especially for two young girls from a quiet, farming community.

Betty got decent grades through school into high school. She worked hard at being a good student. While she was very quiet in class and around her country school, staying in the background most of the time, she was slowly coming out of her shell. No way did she want to seem aggressive or forward like Virginia. She was going to be proper and not draw attention to herself. The same held true at any social function. Betty would hold back, slightly smile, keeping her hands folded together. *I'm the good girl* she would think to herself. *Mama and Papa know that, and it makes me special.* Virginia did well enough in school but always had discipline problems. Following the rules was not an easy road for her. *I am not going to be forced to do what I don't want to* would pop in her mind when authority figures were around.

While Betty was fuller figured, Virginia always "maintained" her slight appearance, and, at sixteen years old and five feet tall, she weighed just seventy-five pounds. One day Janie noticed the girl was losing weight, asking her, "Do you feel ok, honey?" "I'm fine, Mom," Virginia would snap back. Little by little, the weight was falling off, the girl hardly eating or skipping meals. Janie found signs of vomit in the toilet. They were convinced Virginia must have some sort of physical ailment, like a bad flu. Raymond kept saying to Janie and Pete, "Something's wrong here, Virginia is looking terrible! You need to get her to a doctor to figure this out."

Not fully understanding how to handle this situation, they did need the prodding. They finally decided to see the local doctor, Virginia fighting not to go yelling "I'm fine, leave me alone!" Not listening, they dragged her to the office and had her examined. They knew the local doctor well, Dr. Roberts, trusting him explicitly. During this time in the 1940s, you never questioned a physician, following every order they gave, never personally researching to give you some sort of background of an ailment. He was a small-town doctor, used to bandaging cuts, wrapping sprained ankles, and taking care of colds and flu. This kind of diagnosis was out of his league, but there was no way he would admit to that or really know the right way to handle this. After all, he was the family doctor with lots of schooling and plaques on his wall to prove it.

After examining her, he announced that Virginia needed psychological help and recommended a facility in a larger city an hour and a half south. Dr. Roberts let them know "She needs to be there at least a week for treatment." He was proud that he came up with this diagnosis and thought, *I am a good doctor. Glad I could help these poor people.* Trusting this man implicitly, they followed his guidance to the letter. Dr. Roberts immediately called the hospital and planned for her stay. He wrote down directions so the family could easily fine the location.

Pete and Janie left with Virginia, got to the ranch, and packed some of her clothes along with personal things for the drive south to the hospital

Dr. Roberts recommended. Betty was in school, and didn't know what had happened till she got back to the ranch and Uncle Raymond filled her in. "Oh, Uncle Raymond, I feel so bad for her," she said, loosely hugging him. But in her mind, she was thinking, *What is the matter with that girl. Always, always trying to get attention!* Pete and Janie were determined to get her the help she needed. This was a couple decades before these symptoms were recognized and diagnosed as bulimia, the mental disorder that affects many people, especially women.

All the way to hospital, Virginia kept saying, "I am ok. I do not want to go to the hospital."

Janie would repeat over and over, "The doctor knows best. You will get better once you're in the hospital with all those smart doctors."

Pete was silent, driving as fast as he could in the ranch pickup truck to get to their hospital destination on the two-lane highway heading south.

Once they arrived, Virginia was determined not to go into the hospital and fought tooth and nail, screaming, "I don't need this. *Please* take me home, I promise I'll be good!" They had to call the men in the white coats to come out and drag Virginia inside, kicking, yelling, and cursing. "You fuckers are going to be sorry for this!" she wailed. Being around working men for years, Virginia knew plenty of cuss words to throw out at everyone.

Even though her poor body was half its usual size, Virginia still had plenty of strength to fight them off. With three orderlies pulling at her, the men got the girl inside and into the examination room. Her parents signed some papers, not realizing what would be happening to their daughter, trusting everyone in this situation. Fortunately, this was a state-run facility at no cost to the family. They left to return to the ranch, thinking this would take care of everything.

During these times, part of treating this type of diagnosed mental illness were shock treatments, along with intense sessions interacting with a psychologist/psychiatrist. The shock treatments were excruciating, with saliva dripping from Virginia's mouth during these sessions. Medication was given to keep her calm, and food was necessary. In the beginning, Virginia would not follow their orders, trying to stay in control. The girl finally realized she needed to give in and let them do their jobs so she could get this over with and go back home, the medication helping her return to the calm part of her personality to save her from further examinations.

After a week, the hospital decided Virginia was cured. She answered all their questions properly, making sure she was not going to be made to stay there any longer. The meds had calmed her down, yet she still had some fight in her. The thing was, she knew she had to keep that rage hidden, as she thought, *They may think they got me, but I'm still in charge!*

Janie and Pete were called, immediately leaving to pick Virginia up. The hospital assured the parents that all would be well from now on. Virginia got into the car, tired, yet calm. They were satisfied, almost happy. This was never talked about again nor thrown in her face. It was as if it never happened. They were good parents and people would see that they cared for their family. That was the important thing.

The reality was that this horrible experience made Virginia even more determined to be in control of her life. The girl convinced herself to play the game, be good, but be strong when she needed to be. This life pattern was the map that drove Virginia to live the way she wanted, at times in chaos. It was *the* roads she chose that could be bumpy as hell, with the decision to go one way rather than the other. As her brain had formed a mantra after her devil experience, Virginia's new mantra was "I am not crazy, and I will not let *them* rule my life! Fuck anyone who tries to not let me be who I am!"

7

FUTURES FORMING

VIRGINIA KEPT HER HEAD DOWN, trying to be as good as possible to show she wasn't crazy. There is no doubt that her interaction with Leroy and her hospital stay added to her mental journey. The experiences were piled up with the other mental fragments the young girl had going on in her brain. Virginia graduated from high school, and then she got a job at a nearby vegetable processing plant. She worked hard, was exceptionally good at her job, and was very proud of that.

Betty had already graduated from high school, having an office job at the same vegetable processing plant as Virginia. As Betty matured, she became more physically beautiful. She was a stunning, natural beauty, looking so much like Elizabeth Taylor you would do a double take to make sure it wasn't the beloved actress. They were almost the same age, and Betty just loved having this natural beauty. With raven hair cut like Elizabeth Taylor's and the same beautiful blue eyes, Betty wore all the current styles that fit her curvy body so well. She loved dresses that belted at her midsection with a full skirt, showing her small waist. She had charge accounts at all the best dress shops and had tons of clothes to wear for any occasion. Betty's days of standing in the background were gone. Everyone loved Betty, family, friends, coworkers; she was always happy, ready to help with whatever you needed. Betty seemed to be always in a good mood, throwing her head back laughing at everyone's jokes, while accepting male advances with a coy, sexy smile, her being the "eye candy" in most situations.

Virginia did not care that Betty worked in the office, adorned with makeup and pretty dresses. Virginia knew she was a much harder worker and could run physical rings around Betty. Virginia even got to oversee the crew on the packing line, charming everyone with those twinkling eyes. She was the happiest she had ever been. She would prove to everyone that she was important in the world. Then she met George, and her world would change forever.

8

CRAZY LOVE

GEORGE WAS TIRED OF OKLAHOMA and ready for a new adventure. His life had been spent in a small town where everyone's business was shared and gossiped about, something he was just plain tired of. The young man was restless and needed to see what the big world had to offer. While George came from solid roots and a well-respected local family who followed the rules and worked hard for what they had, George had become the renegade of the family. He just couldn't follow the family pattern, and trouble seemed to follow him wherever he went. He was always drinking with his friends, partying, and doing what he wanted rather than being a productive part of the community. George and his best friend from childhood, Sam, would be the ones that got in the most trouble, even robbing a small store just because they were bored and felt like it. The excitement gave George such an adrenaline high that his desire was to keep living this way. But after a while, their continued brush with the law got old. George and Sam decided it was time to hit the railway freight lines close by and get out of town. That world was waiting, and they needed to be out there and experience it.

While George came from a strong, familial heritage, Sam had a much different background. He and his mother, Lucinda, were what the locals referred to as "trailer trash," that unflattering description of people that didn't have the same breaks as others, or just did not care. His mother had gotten pregnant with him at sixteen. The father was a drifter that filled her head with dreams of living in the big city. After a couple of months, he was on his way and never looked back. She never told him she was pregnant, and Lucinda had the baby some months later, her family's shame causing them to turn their backs on her. She did love her baby she'd named Sam, and knew she had to get to work to take care of him. She got a job at Harps Grocery Store and kept that job for years, living in a trailer on the outskirts of town. It was the only thing she could afford and grew to have friends in the park that embraced her and Sam. Lucinda did the best she could with Sam, but that boy was wild and hard to tame. Constantly in trouble, she was glad when he wanted to see the states with his best friend, hoping nothing bad would happen to him. George's family was not thrilled and did their best to stop him from this crazy adventure. It was a waste of their time. Once George got something in his head, that was it.

They each grabbed a bag of necessary things: clothes, personal items, some food. They headed out for a new adventure across the states, maybe to California where they heard there were opportunities with lots of good paying jobs. Oklahoma had fared ok after the Great Depression and World War II, but it was time to make a change. The world was waiting for them to make their mark. Away they went, jumping on the next freight train on which they could sneak onto. The guys had a little money they got from family, but that had to last. They were on their own to get jobs and make more money to live…and (hopefully) prosper.

Their travels led George and Sam through many states, all types of weather, all types of terrain. It was exhilarating for these guys, small-town young men exploring the world, thinking they were big shots. When the railway led them to a California coastal town, they jumped off the train and yelled, "We're not afeared of hard work, we made it to California!" The guys heard there were jobs at vegetable packing plants right in this little town where acres of land grew a huge number of vegetables that needed bodies to help pack and ship them. They got jobs right away, working on the packing line at a plant—the same plant where Virginia and Betty worked. It wasn't long before sparks started to fly between George and Virginia, the young lady ready for anyone who gave her the masculine attention she so wanted.

George had that Elvis look, suave, greased back hair, with that typical, slow Oklahoma "twang" voice. Virginia immediately fell in love with this bad boy, his know-it-all strut, along with his "salesman" way of talking that would mesmerize anyone in his vicinity. This was it for Virginia, her ticket out of the small town that had gossiped about her, just as George's town had done to him. She let George whisk her away from the clutches of her family, and their crazy journey began. *I will live my life the way I want to!* she thought. *This will show* them *I am a person who has her own life to live and somebody to love her!* At twenty-five and nineteen years old, George and Virginia ran off and got married by the local justice of the peace. She chose the road she wanted, with the years showing it was much bumpier than she could have ever imagined. Their journey of a tumultuous relationship was off and running.

9

CHAOS BIRTH

Virginia wanted to move away from her family, and George agreed. They decided to move to a southern area of California, where Sam ended up as well. They both worked odd jobs to keep money coming in, renting a single-wide mobile home. Life was good, Virginia was free of her family, on her own, and did not give a crap about them. George loved her, and that is all she needed.

The young couple loved to party, George being a happy drunk in the beginning. They would have fun drinking, dancing, having a good ole time with Sam and their new group of friends. Then the drunker George got, the meaner he became. The man would get sloppy drunk, and with Virginia's own mean streak, they would get into huge fights. There were many times George gave Virginia a severe beating, once ending up with a broken arm. Emergency trips to the hospital were common. Of course, he would immediately say, "I am so sorry, baby. You know I love ya!" the usual recanting of an abusive alcoholic. Viginia would tell the hospital that she ran into the door or slipped and fell coming out of the trailer door. Anything to keep her man out of jail.

Then Virginia got pregnant. She was fearful of what might happen to the baby if she stayed with George during the pregnancy, afraid his drinking would not stop, and he would hit her and hurt the baby. She called Janie, begging to let her come home while she was pregnant, then to have the baby, staying indefinitely. Pete and Janie jumped at the chance to have her back. Keeping Virginia and their grandchild safe was the most important thing, and everything else was forgiven.

She traveled up by Greyhound bus, arriving a few months pregnant. Virginia felt safe at the ranch with her parents taking the best care of her. All Pete and Janie cared about was that Virginia was safely at home, with their new grandchild on the way. They had no idea about the abuse their daughter had experienced yet they knew there had to be a reason she wanted to come home. It was better for them not to ask and just be happy they could enjoy this experience. Betty was glad her sister was home, knowing full well this would happen, thinking, *Why does she have to make a mess of her life when she has such a loving family?*

It was March 1954, and spring had just begun. Virginia was feeling huge as her due date had passed and she just needed to get this baby out of her, being her usual impatient self. Standing in the ranch kitchen, looking out at the fields of an early crop of newly planted corn, she heard a splatter of water and looked down to see a puddle between her feet. She let out a blood-curdling scream, yelling, "Someone help me, my water broke!" Hearing this, Janie stopped folding clothes in her bedroom and called out the window to Pete who was in the yard between milking times. They got her things together for the hospital, jumped in Pete's pickup, and drove her as fast as they could to the Catholic hospital in town.

It ended up being a quick birth, and Virginia's sweet baby girl was born. The hospital was a few miles into town, rising three stories above the meadowy fields heading east to the low range of hills that created the valley the town nestled in. The family had all sorts of ideas about names, chiming in with this one or that. No way would Virginia entertain any of *their* ideas. "I'll name my baby anything I want," she announced.

Looking out her window at the beautiful meadows just behind the hospital, Virginia said, "Baby, I want to name you Meadow. They will not like it, but too bad. You are my baby!" With Mary, Susan, Deborah, and other names being much more common during the 1950s, Virginia got her way for her little girl to have a different name. Virginia loved that fact; it was one more way of showing she could be in charge, not bowing to her family's wishes.

During the pregnancy, George had moved back with his family to Oklahoma, while Sam stayed in the LA area. Trouble continually followed Sam, the man ending up getting arrested for armed robbery. Sam was one of those "they ain't gonna get me!" guys who just could not keep his mouth shut. He was awaiting trial in the LA County jail and mouthed off to the wrong person. The guy was part of a local Mexican gang that got arrested for murdering a young girl. They briefly ended up in the same cell and Sam spit on his cellmate, calling him a "damn spic." The guy was huge with a beastly temper and beat Sam to death. Hearing the ruckus, the guards made their way into the cell to pull the man off Sam. Seeing what they saw scared them into slow motion as they realized their help was of no use. They slowly unlocked the gate and pulled the strong man off Sam. It was too late, Sam's face smashed in, ribs broken, his lifeless body lying there in a pool of blood. Hoping for good news from this call from LA, Lucinda was devastated when the jailer called that Sam was gone. With no money to bury her son, the county cremated his remains and spread them in a vacant field, saying a few words regarding his soul. When she told her friends about her loss, they told her how sorry they were, thinking, *What did you expect from that no-good loser?!* No matter what, her heart was broken, and she blamed herself for his misguided life.

George kept calling Virginia, begging her to come back to him. He was lonely, telling her how much he loved her, and that the drinking would stop. He wanted to see his new baby girl. When Meadow was six months old, Virginia finally gave in, announcing to the family, "I'm going to take Meadow and go back with George to Oklahoma. We love each other! He's promised to change, and I know he will this time." Realizing the relationship turmoil that would happen, Pete and Janie looked at each other and said, "You can leave if you want. But you are *not* taking our sweet Meadow with you!" With that determined look in her eyes, Virginia gave in, leaving Meadow with her family. In the back of her mind, she knew this was the best thing. The crazy and passionately deranged love between George and Virginia had won out one more time.

Pete drove Virginia to the local Greyhound bus station and dropped her off, suitcase in hand. They smiled and said their goodbyes, his sad eyes telling a different story. Her life flashed through his mind. A life that had been difficult for everyone, with regret that he hadn't done things differently, with more love, guidance, and understanding. These regrets he carried for the rest of his life. Sadly, he watched the bus pull out of the station. He wondered if he would ever see Virginia again.

10

ROMANCE TRAVELS

GEORGE'S FAMILY EMBRACED VIRGINIA. THEY loved their son and daughter-in-law, wanting their life to turn around and be productive parts of society. These were another set of good, hardworking people, like Pete and Janie. The idea that they could not see Meadow crushed them. This family had hope that someday they could be a part of the girl's life. Virginia and George lived with his parents and got jobs in the local town, trying to make another go of it. They had all the support they needed from his family and should have just stayed and given their relationship the time it needed to mature. Virginia quickly became pregnant, having another baby girl they named Jean. Although they had Meadow in their hearts, this was a second chance at making a life together.

The winter weather in this part of Oklahoma is severe, with lots of rain, snow, winds, and tornadoes. The conditions were much different from the medium-temperate climate Virginia was used to on the California coast. Virginia complained to George much of the time about the weather and how she wanted to be closer to their first baby, Meadow. She would never admit it, but she also missed her California family. "George, please let's move back to California," she'd plead. "I promise things will work out with my family. We will get to see our sweet Meadow and be a part of her life." George was reluctant but wanted to make Virginia happy. He too was tired of the cold, winter weather; being part of Meadow's life was as important to him as it was to Virginia. He figured if things did not work out in California, the family of four could move back and be part of the Oklahoma lifestyle.

Virginia made the call home. It was tough to do, knowing full well she might get a verbal lashing for leaving her child. The only time she called her parents from Oklahoma was when she had gotten off the bus, quickly getting to a pay phone, letting them know that she had arrived safely. There had been no connection with Betty. Virginia knew full well how judgmental she would be about the situation of choosing George over her child.

Janie answered and Virginia sweetly asked if she could talk to her Papa, knowing full well he was an easy sell. Pete wanted her back close to them, trying to recapture the closeness he let go of years ago. They would have to accept George as part of the deal. That is the way it was. And the new grandbaby Jean was a huge plus in the couple returning.

What George and Virginia did not know was that Pete, Janie, and Betty had already gone to an attorney and received legal custody of Meadow. They were not about to subject this beautiful child to the chaotic life her parents lived. Naturally, Betty was the instigator of the legal proceedings, hiring the attorney and getting her parents to go along with the plan. This was a power she silently held over her sister for the rest of their lives, becoming the adult that demanded Virginia follow the rules, just as Betty had followed Patrick's rules. Going before the judge, it was a simple process to get him to sign the papers. With George's drinking history and Virginia's mental records, and the fact that they had left the baby, it was easy for the judge to finalize this legal proceeding. Giving the grandparents custody of Meadow was the best thing the judge could do. Betty was the continued driving force in getting her parents' legal guardianship of Meadow. She emphatically told her parents, "No way is my sister capable of raising this child; Meadow needs us!"

Pete and Janie had recently bought a small rental house in the larger town as an investment. Janie's thrifty ways and hard work at the ranch enabled her to save and purchase the house. The house was between renters and was the perfect size for the family of three to move into. The 900-square-foot house, painted yellow with white trim, was in a well-kept, modest neighborhood. Being the perfect size, the house had two bedrooms, one bathroom, a kitchen, dining room, and living area. The kitchen had 1950s appliances: a white O'Keefe and Merritt stove, a white porcelain sink with two sides, and a General Motors refrigerator with the "steering wheel" handle. The one car garage was perfect for the cars of the 1950s, with room for a washing machine. The backyard was good size. It was divided into two sections by a low, white picket fence. The first, a lawn area with flowering plants all around the edge and a clothesline for drying clothes. The second, an orchard of fruit trees that included apple, peach, and lemon. The ground around the trees was raked dirt, meticulously kept. Outside the kitchen door (to the right) was a lattice covered patio that was perfect for those warm California days.

George, Virginia, and Baby Jean traveled back to California and moved into the house. Fortunately, it came furnished so moving in was a breeze. George got a job delivering linens to restaurants and event locations, while Virginia was a stay-at-home mom, trying to make amends for not being there for Meadow. This family now had another chance at living a fulfilling life.

Once Pete and Janie got custody of Meadow, Betty went into full-swing parenting mode. It didn't matter that her parents had legal guardianship, Betty was going to make sure things went the way she wanted. There was no way this girl was turning out like her mother: unstable, defiant, crazy. Janie would make sure Meadow followed rules, but Betty knew that Janie and Pete would not be as strict as they should be with the girl. The disciplinarian in Betty slowly emerged, a force so strong that the grandparents could not stop it. *Meadow will be a good, smart girl* she told herself. *I will do whatever it takes to make sure of that!*

Meadow, Virginia, Pete, and Janie got the brunt end of everything. Betty would berate them for this or that, belittling at every turn. Unfortunately, they did not have the tools to stop her and fight back. Once Virginia moved back home, she would then recoil like a wounded animal around Betty. Meadow was too young to know how. Pete and Janie trusted Betty, as she was smarter and more educated than them. Following Betty's lead seemed like the only thing to do.

Pete and Janie loved and cared for Meadow. Some might say they spoiled her. It was just that Betty's presence ruled them and their decisions—unless they kept things from her, which would happen once they understood the situation. Betty worked a good portion of her adult life thirty miles away by where much of the extended family lived. The ranch was still home, driving to and from work every day. It seemed that Betty chose this situation rather than living on her own to keep tabs on Meadow. Betty's fear of making her own life kept her tied to this routine. It was as if she couldn't allow herself her own happiness, needing to live through others to show her value. If diagnosed, she would be labeled a victim of "Martyr Syndrome," sacrificing her own needs to the benefit of others. Appearances were everything, a fact that continually ruled her direction in life.

11

TRAGIC BOOZING

ONE DAY JEAN WAS IN her bassinet in the small dining room, sleeping with a soft warm summer breeze coming through the window. She was ten months old and the happiest baby, sweet and content. Although George had promised to stop drinking as much, his alcohol disease would not let him slow down. This day, George was off work and started his drinking early, throwing back whiskey like it was water. Virginia yelled, "Can't you stop that drinking for a day?!" George drunkenly got himself up off the couch, walked over to his small-framed wife in the kitchen, and hauled off and slapped her. Knowing what this could lead to, Virginia ran to the phone and called Pete and Raymond at the ranch, screaming for help. Raymond grabbed a baseball bat, and they jumped in their pickup and drove as fast as they could to the house.

Virginia ran to the backyard orchard, trying to escape that inner rage George had. The man was five-foot-ten and weighed 160 pounds versus Virginia's small frame coming in at five feet and 110 pounds. There was no contest on who would win this fight. The two wrestled to the ground. George started choking Virginia, dirt flying everywhere as she violently kicked her feet. Her screaming was muffled by the tight grip on her neck. Her eyes were bulging, and the life was draining out of her.

Pete and Raymond screeched into the driveway and made their way into the house. Looking around, they wondered where the two could be. Then they heard the commotion in the backyard and ran out there, kicking open the screen door, tearing the screen off. Raymond had a temper like no other if you were doing harm to someone he loved. George was still on top of Virginia. Raymond raised the bat and banged George on the head. George let out a yell you could hear for miles, then jumped up, his fists ready for a fight. Raymond yelled, "Oh no you don't. One more move and I'll do you in!"

George put his fists down and just stood there. The smell of alcohol was enough to knock you out from the fumes. Virginia started fully breathing. Slowly Pete and Raymond pulled her up. "Are you ok, honey?" Pete asked. "I'll survive, Papa. I know he loves me, but when he's drinking that devil part of him just comes out, and it's hard to stop." The devil image of Leroy in her adolescent dream quickly flashed in her mind, then was gone just as quick.

George just stood there, blood coming out from the back of his head, saying, "You know I love ya, baby. You just can't keep dat mouth shut!" George started to give her a hug. Virginia backed off. George started to fall over as she moved out of his way, but he steadied himself before he fell. Pete and Raymond pulled him into the house and looked at the wound on his head. "You'll survive," Raymond said. "I'm not wasting a trip to the hospital on you!" Pete cleaned up his wound, deciding what to do about the situation, not including George in the conversation.

They decided to get George a motel room for the night to keep the couple separate. George could figure out in the morning how to get back to the house. The motel was only five blocks away on the main street of the town. "You can walk back to the house. And if you touch her again, that bat will do more damage than just a bloody bump on the head!" Pete said as Raymond shoved George into the pickup, and they took off.

Virginia dragged herself into the house, almost forgetting about Jean. She quickly remembered to check on the baby and went into the dining room where Jean was, that gentle breeze and afternoon light still coming through the sheer curtains. "Oh baby, I'm so sorry for all the yelling," Virginia said as she walked up to the bassinet.

Virginia assumed Jean was sleeping. She bent down to kiss her but noticed she didn't feel warm. Jean wasn't breathing, her lifeless body calm, serene. The baby looked like an angel who was preserved in time. Virginia let out a blood-curdling scream, grabbed the lifeless baby, and rushed her to the hospital in her '55 two-door blue-and-white Chevy Pete had bought for them. She drove like a maniac through the town heading east to the hospital, the same place she had given birth to Meadow, and where Leroy had been stitched up. She was crying so hard she could barely see. Not only had she been beaten and choked by George, but her baby girl was in trouble!

Virginia ran into the emergency room with Jean, yelling at the top of her lungs, "Help me *please*!! My baby's in trouble!!" The nurse rushed Jean into the operatory to the doctors on staff. They tried to resuscitate the baby, but they knew immediately it was of no use, going through the motions to make sure appearances seemed accurate. This sad occurrence was blamed on something the doctors had seen before: spontaneous death of a baby for no reason, a decade later described as crib death syndrome. The family could not help but think that the fight between Virginia and George was to blame, just one more thing to pack into her already fragile mind.

Her cycle of shame, blame, and psychosis continued for years, accentuating her defiant nature. The events of her first child legally being taken away by her family and her second child dying in her care, tragically defined her life, allowing her psychosis to manifest itself in different ways. Continual blame from everyone fueled Virginia's rage to be different, never allowing anyone to tell her what to do from that day forward. She promised herself, *I will do what I want, when I want—those fuckers will not rule my life.*

12

FINAL REST

GEORGE HAD NO IDEA THAT Baby Jean had passed away. He slept hard and long after his drinking binge. Getting up, he had a throbbing headache, and his memory was a bit cloudy. This wasn't new to him. There were many times he landed somewhere without remembering how he got there. But this time, he did. Feeling just a bit guilty, he got up, put on his clothes, and checked himself out in the mirror. George had that James Dean in *Rebel Without a Cause* look with his white short-sleeve T-shirt and jeans, and nonfilter Camel cigarettes rolled up in his shirt sleeve. He wanted to be that nonconformist: cool, rebellious, no one telling him what to do, just like the movie's character, Jim Stark. That trait was at the root of most of their arguments. Virginia would try to "boss him around," especially when he had been drinking. That always got them going at each other.

"I look cool," he said aloud. Except that his shirt had blood stains on it, which he did not give a crap about. He was sure he fought back hard, no shame in that. Wearing a belt with his Levi jeans, George cinched it tight with his shirt tucked in. He got his dark hair wet and pushed it back with his hand, feeling the wound on his head, now remembering things more vividly. "There, ya dumb fuck, ain't lookin' so bad." He left the motel and started walking the five blocks back to the house. The sun was hot, so his hair dried quickly. As he walked up to the house, all the family cars were there, and he thought, *Fuck, what the heck now?*

Knowing he was going to be slaughtered by everyone for his behavior, he slowly opened the screen door, ready for the barrage of verbal attacks he thought would happen. To his surprise, everyone was sitting around. They barely looked up at him. Then he saw Virginia and she ran up to him crying, "George, our Baby Jean passed away." Tears were streaming down her cheeks.

Not understanding what she was saying, he just stood there with a look of bewilderment. "What do ya mean about the baby?" was all he could come up with. She explained as best she could about going back into the house to check on Jean after the fight. George immediately started to blame Virginia, and then he realized he had better console without attacking anyone. He was in no position to judge Virginia right now, especially after the previous day's happenings.

The family was aware of their fight. That was the least of their concerns right now, they had a funeral to think about. They all decided to have a small service at the mausoleum where they would purchase a crypt for Baby Jean as they did for the other members of the family in the small town about a half hour north where much of Pete and Janie's family lived. It was a beautiful place. The floors were white marble with benches set in the center at various positions in the long halls of the mausoleum. It was full of light and not one bit depressing—a comfortable place for Baby Jean to be laid to rest. It was somewhere to visit her, to remember her brief life. Each crypt had a name plaque with a brass metal hanger that held a small vase for their loved ones to place flowers.

Betty included Meadow in all of this. She wanted her to understand about dying, the reality of death in life. Meadow was expected to be quiet and poised, no questions asked. Meadow was only four at the time and truly could not grasp the effect this had on everyone. She was confused and had not understood where Baby Jean had come from in the first place. Her parents had come back, but Meadow still did not live with them. The confusion continued, with Betty dragging Meadow around to anything that happened because of the Baby Jean situation. Janie wanted Meadow to stay with someone instead of attending the funeral, because she knew it just was not right—Meadow was too little to understand. "She needs to get used to it, Mama," Betty smartly responded. "It is life. She needs to learn respect for the dead!"

What was going through Betty's mind was herself having to attend funerals when she was a little girl, so scared of the unknown but forced to attend out of respect. Respect that Pete and Janie instilled in her. Meadow was not going to escape this experience no matter what. Betty thought, *Mama and Papa just spoil this girl. No way is she getting out of this! I had to go through it, now she must.*

The impulse to control this child and not giving her a break from discipline was all that Aunt Betty cared about. Whatever experiences Betty learned from, Meadow would as well. She believed that Meadow would be a better person for it.

They held funeral service, and Baby Jean was laid to rest in her crypt. Jean's name was added to the plaque on her little space along with her birthdate, and date of death. A follow-up reception was held at Pete's mother's house in the small town where the mausoleum was for friends and family to attend. She had moved there a few years previous, not long after her husband died, leaving their ranch for in town living. Meadow got lots of hugs, asking how she was. Articulate for sure, she would respond, "I feel happy. My sister Jean is asleep in that pretty place. I can go see her anytime."

Aunt Betty had coached Meadow to answer in the way she thought Meadow should. Even though she said the words, Meadow didn't understand what all this meant. She knew her parents had come back in her life. They had a new baby they doted on, and they were giving Meadow some attention. But she did not live with them and only saw them at times. Meadow loved the baby when she saw her, touching her cheeks and giving her a kiss on her little forehead. Baby Jean seemed like a doll to Meadow. A doll that came to life, like a toy rather than a little sister. And now she was gone.

13

RELATIONSHIP DEMISE

FTER THIS TRAGEDY, GEORGE AND Virginia's addictive love/hate romance gave them one more chance to forgive each other. This repeated theme of drink, argue, hurt had to stop for their relationship *and* personal survival. Being in the house where their baby Jean had just died kept the memory of the whole situation at the forefront of their minds. George needed to get back home where he could be loved by his family, a place where he could feel safe and not judged by Virginia's family—especially Betty, who was the judge and jury for anything Virginia did.

George was reluctant to ask Virginia, but he decided he needed to bring this up: "Baby, this California ain't workin' out for us. Let's go back to Oklahoma where we can be loved by my family." Heartbroken, with no one else to turn to, Virginia agreed. *This will work for sure*, George thought. *She'll not be such a crazy bitch to me when she's aways from that family, and I'll slow down this dang drinkin' of mine…*

While his family loved Virginia and George and were happy to have them back in Oklahoma, neither Virginia nor George could seem to keep it together. Like anyone who has the disease of alcoholism, he still drank, becoming that mean drunk Virginia knew all too well. She would fight back, they'd make up, and the cycle would continue. Then, Virginia got pregnant again. The pregnancy was a product of George getting drunk, becoming that crazed being she was so afraid of, just letting him have "his way" with her. It was rape, Virginia never consenting, knowing she just needed to let George have what he wanted to keep him from physically hurting her. She kept the pregnancy a secret, knowing George would be more upset with her now than ever.

She hadn't mentioned the pregnancy to anyone, which was easily hidden under her coat and loose clothes in the winter season. This part of Oklahoma is full of trees and beautiful, but again, with tough winters. When George noticed her tummy was bigger, he said, "What the hell is wrong with your stomach?!" Virginia's only reply was a meek, "I don't know, it might be one of those tumor things."

George's younger brother, Elliot, was his go-to for anything that required brains. Elliot was the smart one in the family, educated and successful. George took Virginia to see Elliot, and he gave him some money to take her to the doctor. As usual, George was broke, and they were living with his parents, who continually enabled this son and always got him out of trouble. They blamed George's mistakes on everyone else, or the time of year, or the economy. Without realizing it, they enabled his cycle of failure to continue by not making him take responsibility for the things that happened in his life. It was the only way they knew how to love him.

George didn't dare worry his mom and dad about anything going on, so the brother was his safest recourse. Virginia knew she must be pregnant but just couldn't bring herself into the reality of the situation. Hiding the pregnancy was driven by the fearful desire to keep George from an angrier attack on her. A quick examination by a local doctor revealed she was five months pregnant. George was livid and said, "We gotta take care of this; no way am I gonna go through havin' another kid." They found out about a doctor in a larger town a few miles away, where she could go into the hospital for a late-term abortion, claiming she couldn't carry the baby for fear of the pregnancy harming her physically. They made the drive to the hospital, got her checked in, and were able to have *the surgery* that day. Complications resulted, and a complete hysterectomy was performed on Virginia, which was probably the best for everyone.

When Virginia got out of the hospital, she was weak and unstable, but George was done—no more of her craziness, their continued yelling and screaming at each other. Their relationship was just over, and he wanted

Virginia gone. He loaded Virginia and her things in his Ford pickup and drove the 1,650-mile trip straight to her parents' ranch house, dropped her off, and said to them, "She's yours."

He turned right around and took off, out of their lives forever. Divorce papers were filed, signed by George, and (reluctantly) Virginia, legally finalizing the end of their marriage. It took some time, but Virginia healed, at least physically. No matter if the web she wove was due to her own doing, the consequences were devastating: she left her Meadow, then lost custody of the baby, and Baby Jean died in her care. The love of her life throws her aside, ending back at the place she desperately wanted to get away from, that place where gossip flowed, and memories were not the kindest to her. With mental wounds as they were, Virginia's life would be changed forever, trying to get her life together, never wanting to go back to that mental hospital she loathed being at. With no place else to go, she stayed with her parents and Meadow during this time, getting her job back at the local vegetable processing plant. She never looked back or blamed herself. The family did enough of that. Along with healing, spending time with her Meadow was the most important thing to Virginia.

14

MEADOW

<hr>

EADOW WAS THE CUTEST, MOST precocious child, petite
with blond hair. She was a little princess in a house filled with
mostly men who were family or workers on the dairy. She
was a ray of sunshine, bringing a glow of happiness where there had been
darker times, both familial and worldwide. This was the 1950s, a peaceful
time of progress, growth, wellbeing, and prosperity that came from the
world surviving the horrors of World War II. There was no question that
obtaining legal custody of Meadow was the right decision to protect her
in Pete and Janie's environment of love and safety.

Meadow would light up a room when she toddled in, jabbering about this
or that. She felt the safest when she laid in Janie's lap, looking up at her
smiling face. Some of Meadow's fondest memories are during this time
of being on the ranch with animals, nature, love. All the working men
adored her and helped care for her when they were called on—especially
Uncle Raymond, who was really her great-uncle, but was considered her
uncle, as were all her great-aunts and -uncles.

Meadow would run out into the alfalfa fields and play hide-and-seek with
her grandmother. Janie pretended she never saw Meadow, loudly saying,
"Where are you honey, are you lost? What if I can't find you?" Thinking
she really couldn't find her, Meadow would yell, in her high little voice,
"I'm right here, grama. Please don't leave me in the field!" Then Janie
would grab her up and snuggle her so close she almost couldn't breathe,
creating a lasting bond for Meadow and Grama Janie.

Meadow loved the moist, cool ocean breeze that came through the yard most days, its refreshing qualities invigorating everything it swept past. Being by the coast, everything grew beautifully in her grandmother's yard. She loved to get her feet and hands dirty being with Grama Janie, working the soil, planting flowers and the vegetables she would use in her cooking. She grew many beautiful varieties of flowers—nasturtiums, sunflowers, roses, stock. It was a fabulous paradise of senses for the young girl, something to have fond memories of for the rest of her life. Janie would stand in the garden, whisk Meadow up in her arms, the sun shining down, and whisper, "We love you so much, Meadow… We are so glad you're here."

Being loved and cherished by her grandparents, Meadow felt protected and safe. Then Betty would arrive, and things would change. "Now you make sure she behaves," Betty would tell Pete and Janie. "We want her to turn out good!" The fear that would creep in was compounded with a slap here and there. At an early age, Meadow learned what can happen if you did not follow her rules. While aware of this, something inside of her kept wanting to test those discipline waters, a bit of *renegade* inheritance from Virginia.

One day at the ranch, Meadow was "helping" her grandmother wash the dishes, while Janie was hanging clothes on the clothesline that overlooked the fields, humming "Bye Bye Love" by the Everly Brothers. All the new rock-and-roll music was becoming popular, and it drew Janie into a different world when she heard it, making the mundane job of hanging clothes more of an event than a chore.

Meadow was up on a kitchen chair with a towel tied around her waist to keep her clothes from getting too wet. The counters were sheets of inexpensive laminate with metal edging, while the floor was simple linoleum, with a sort of "splattered" stone look, popular during this time. Fortunately, the sink was thick white porcelain and cleaned up easily. This was a fun time for Meadow, and nothing would be hurt by water and soap spilling over on these kitchen staples, with cleanup taking only a few minutes.

Meadow was splashing and playing, washing a dish here and there. Aunt Betty walked in early from work, looking over at the sink as she set her purse down on the large kitchen table. Gasping, she yelled "Meadow!" The little three-year-old was startled, with her eyes opening as wide as they could. The coffee mug she was washing slipped out of her hand, hitting the floor and shattering into small pieces everywhere. Meadow's body tensed briefly, then Aunt Betty grabbed Meadow, shaking the poor girl as she yelled, "What are you doing?! That is not how you wash dishes!" Meadow was stiff with fear and couldn't say a word, tears of fear starting to run down her pink cheeks. Betty then slapped her. "Never do this again or you'll be sent to your room without supper!"

Betty let go of Meadow. Then from behind came Raymond, grabbing Betty, turning her around, giving her a slap as well. "Don't hurt that little girl, she's only three!" Stunned, Betty grabbed her purse and went into the bathroom, while Meadow ran crying to the safety of her bed. Hearing the commotion, Janie ran in and stood in the kitchen doorway watching. It was as if this was taking place in slow motion, almost like a movie. Janie was in shock but had to let things go the way they did. Raymond was a strong force at the ranch, and she never went against him. *Betty's just trying to help*, she thought and went over to sink to begin the cleanup. Then a rage came up inside Janie that wanted to help her dear Meadow, trying to figure out what to do. But then she just went about her business, cleaning up the soapy mess, leaving the situation as it was. She thought, *Betty knows what's best.*

After a bit, Betty went into their bedroom to give Meadow a stern talking to. Betty would stay there at night and weekends to keep an eye on things, her self-appointed job in action. Cowering a bit in her bed, Meadow was so scared she almost wet her pants—pants that were still wet as Betty wouldn't let her change yet. Seeing this, Aunt Betty toned it down a bit, but she still felt she had to reinforce how to behave. "Now Meadow, splashing water all over is not right. If you're washing dishes, you do it slowly to make sure they are clean and put neatly on the counter for drying. Am I making myself clear?" Meadow shook her head *yes*; not understanding all this, she just wanted to change her clothes. Betty gave Meadow a little slap on the cheek just to make sure the girl understood. They changed her and the sheets, Betty acting as if nothing happened.

This was the reoccurring theme of discipline: Meadow would do something not to Betty's liking. Betty would reprimand Meadow by yelling at her; slapping her; or sending her to their room to get beat with a coat hanger on her little naked butt. Talking back, not following rules, making a mess playing were all things that warranted Betty's strict discipline protocol. Betty would make sure Raymond wasn't around during these times. "He doesn't have children; how could he know how they should be raised?" she'd mumble to herself.

Betty's goal was to instill in Meadow to have respect for her life, reinforcing that without her grandparents and her Aunt Betty, Meadow would be on the streets for sure, with no one to care for her. This constant threat did work to keep Meadow in line. It's just that sometimes she needed to revolt a bit, not too much, but just enough to test the discipline waters. Then, *bam*, she'd get whatever was on the menu that day in discipline, paying for the lapse in judgment.

This was Betty's way of letting out her own demons after putting on a show for everyone daily, being perfect, selfless Betty. Meadow was trapped, and only a few in the outside world would believe she was being treated this way. So, she took it, with a subtle hatred and disgust for Aunt Betty growing inside Meadow over the years. This fact continually fought with the other part of Meadow, the part that was taught to *respect your elders, follow the rules.* The respect part of her psyche would continually win out, keeping their family life on enough of a level platform, not causing internal family conflict…until an Aunt Betty episode would return.

15

CONFIDANT MARY

——————

"**I** KNOW SHE'S MEAN," MEADOW RESPONDED. "But she is my aunt, and she knows that I need to behave. I cannot turn out like my crazy mom and dad." Mary was telling Meadow repeatedly that Aunt Betty was a mean witch and she needed to get back at her some way. "Let's think of something that will hurt her and make her stop," said Mary. Although she was small, Mary was strong-willed and capable of anything. She was Meadow's savior and had helped her so much in the past. Without her, Meadow would not have survived her childhood years. Mary was there no matter what had happened, listening attentively for hours on end in Meadow's room.

The toy area of the bedroom was not large, but it was big enough to hold the minimal amount of playthings Meadow had: the doll, a plastic tea set, blocks, and a few marbles. Her prized possession was her doll confidant, Mary. She carried her around the ranch, making sure she was clean, never getting muddy like Meadow did. Mary's dress was like some of the clothes Aunt Betty had bought Meadow—a frilly dress and socks, with small patent-leather shoes. She had bright eyes and was always smiling; she had a happy face when things weren't very happy. Mary would come to life and carry on the needed conversations with Meadow, trying the very best she could. She knew the score with Aunt Betty's severe discipline methods and if she could just get Meadow to listen, they'd be rid of her.

Janie heard Meadow talking in the bedroom. She stopped her cooking, wiped her hands on her apron, and walked down the hall to Meadow's room. "Honey, who are you talking to?" Janie asked. Meadow quickly answered, "Me and Mary are having a chat." Meadow had picked up words like "chat" as she was around adults all the time. She was like a sponge when it came to language. Meadow added, "She's so nice and really loves me."

Janie replied, "Ok, I'm just making sure no one was coming through the window to get you!"

Janie snickered and thought giving Meadow a little scare was cute. Meadow did giggle but it scared her so much when Janie said things like that. Her insides melted, but at least she had Mary to keep her safe. "Say 'hi' to Mary for me," Janie said as she went back to her cooking. She was smiling and thinking how cute Meadow and her doll were.

"What the heck is she trying to do, my Meadow, scare you to death?! You know you're safe with me, so never mind her," the trusted doll said, right on track with her Meadow defense. Meadow replied, "Grama Janie loves me and would never hurt me, not like Aunt Betty. She loves to tease me." Mary replied, "Doesn't she know these kinds of things scare you?" Mary could not understand this type of love, especially for her Meadow. "I will be ok. Remember: I have you!" Meadow emphatically replied.

Mary kept Meadow safe, spanning from when she was three to about ten years old, somehow finally getting lost or accidentally thrown away. When Aunt Betty was around, Mary would be on guard to help Meadow with anything. After severe discipline, something with hangers or belts, Mary was livid and had to have a stern talk with Meadow—not mean stern but enough to make her listen. Mary said, "Meadow, we need to do something about this mean, witchy bitch." "I know," Meadow responded to Mary, "but she takes care of me and without her I don't know where I'd be." "Well, I'm here to listen and help. You are my friend, and you can hug me, kiss me, and I'm not going anywhere. I'm your savior from all of this!" Mary softly assured the little girl. Then, she kissed Meadow, telling her everything would be ok.

The back-and-forth with Mary was constant. She was a necessary cheerleader for Meadow, keeping Meadow's brain from going to the dark side. Betty would never let Meadow take the doll out of the house, in the car, or traveling wherever they would go. "That doll is a house toy," Betty would say, "you don't need to drag her everywhere you go like those other girls who look like ragamuffins and don't have me and your grandparents to care for them like we do you."

Meadow would plead and plead, but Aunt Betty was not giving in. The girl would know when to stop just before getting a slap. So, Meadow would act like the doll was with her, secretly talking to Mary when she needed to feel safe. Even if the conversation was in Meadow's head, it was enough to keep her happy that her friend was somewhere around close by—anywhere and at any time—her safety net of sanity.

Meadow's need for Mary to travel everywhere she went was a bit confusing for Betty. *Why does she want a doll when she has her grandparents and me to love and protect her?* For an instant she had a fleeting thought that maybe a doll could be a good companion for a young girl, something to confide in with no judgment. She then let the repressed memory of the *encounter* with working man Patrick leak into her mind, thinking how a "Mary" might have been helpful to confide in. Then she thought, *NO… I was strong, I did what I was told and never need to share that with anyone. Virginia and I did not have dolls and did not need them!*

16

VACATION ESCAPE

———

URING THEIR DRIVE FROM OKLAHOMA, neither George nor Virginia spoke a word. He barely would stop for her to go to the bathroom. The man's determination to get his wife back to her California home and out of his life was his driven goal. Every few states Virginia would start to say, "Can't we…" and he'd stop her so quick, she'd slump down in fear. Finally, they got to the ranch, George practically throwing Virginia out of the truck. Demeaning and scary as this was, she had to pick up her things and force herself to walk in the house. She cried all the way inside, with Pete and Janie trying to console her. That part of her life was over. She had to start thinking about herself and the future, beginning the healing from all the tragedy she experienced in the last few years.

Virginia's days were spent living at the ranch trying to survive. This last pregnancy experience, the abortion and surgery, wreaked more havoc on her psyche and body. And while she needed to heal, she was determined to get her job back at the vegetable processing plant and start to rebuild her life. She had no idea where her life was going to lead. What she did know was that she would love her little Meadow, trying her best to be a mom to her. This was not an easy feat with Betty coming around, putting her ideas of behavior onto Meadow, taking over discipline to make sure she became a "quality" human being. With all the things that had happened, Virginia knew she was on thin ice with the family. Yet she was determined to put the past behind her and move on. Her history of severe trauma couldn't be pushed down forever, further enabling her psychosis with hallucinations, erratic behavior, and a need to be the individual trying to get the most attention no matter what the cost.

One day Virginia heard George's voice in her head, telling her he was going to come from Oklahoma and steal Meadow away. At first, she dismissed this, then, his voice would repeatedly say, "I'm comin' for my Meadow," the voice getting louder each time, his Oklahoma twang more pronounce than ever. Over the years, these hallucinations led the people around Virginia to think she was constantly lying. Virginia wasn't lying. She believed these situations were true, because they were reality in her life, added symptoms of her schizophrenia and bipolar disorders. They were lifelong conditions that continually ruled her being, haunting her and others for many years.

She convinced her family that she needed to take Meadow to Aunt Frances's house for safety from her alcoholic, thieving father, George. Virginia excitedly told Meadow, "Baby, we're going to have a fun trip to go see Aunt Frances in San Francisco! I know you love her, and she loves us… We'll have a great time!" Meadow was excited and felt it would be a fun time visiting family without Aunt Betty whispering in her ear to behave or constantly correcting her. It was a huge relief that no coat hangers could be brought out to threaten Meadow with. Or worse yet, spanked with.

While Betty at first tried to stop this trip, the fear of George stealing Meadow seemed real to her as well. After all, Virginia had said that he called and was planning to drive to California and take Meadow back to Oklahoma for a visit. Meadow was his daughter, and George didn't care who had legal custody of the girl. Betty backed off and trusted her Aunt Frances to take good care of them. In a relationship that Betty had most control over, it seems strange that she would not fight Virginia on all of this. The fact was, if Aunt Frances felt George was a real threat, then he must have been. Betty thought, *Aunt Frances is rich and lives in a penthouse, for God's sake, so she must know about all these things, right?* Little did Betty know that Virginia and Meadow were Aunt Frances's favorites. Frances was one of the few that knew how Betty treated Meadow and wanted to save Meadow from Betty's strict rule for as long as she could.

This lady was the smartest one in the family, revered for her style and city living.

Frances was Meadow's great-aunt, Pete's youngest sister. Frances's husband was Larry, and the whole family adored him. Larry owned car dealerships in the Bay Area and seemed quite wealthy. Rumor had it that he had his hands in illegal goings on, but no one knew for sure. They lived in the largest townhome across from the Palace of Fine Arts in San Francisco, which was very exclusive and so different from anything the rest of the family knew. Aunt Frances treated the family so well, giving them all kinds of gifts over the years, and she had a special place in her heart for Virginia and Meadow. Aunt Frances was the perfect person to go visit on a trip. She would welcome them with arms wide open and show them the time of their lives.

So off they went on this little excursion in Virginia's Chevy that Pete had kept at the ranch, oil changed, car washed. He gave them some cash for food and snacks for the five-hour drive north, with beautiful scenery for Meadow to see on the way. Without Aunt Betty around, Meadow could bring Mary, to keep by her side, enjoying this "special" journey as well.

Meadow was a bit nervous during the drive but relaxed more when Virginia let her open the car window, letting the fresh air blow on her face and through her golden locks. *Oh, I love this freedom,* Meadow thought. *Aunt Betty would never allow this!* While she did love her mom, Virginia scared her at times, spouting off this and that, talking to someone who wasn't there. Then Virginia would stop and say to her, "I love you, Meadow," and all seemed well again. These small outbursts were scary for the little girl. Then Meadow would sit back and tell herself and her trusted friend Mary, *She's saving us from my mean dad.* That would make her feel safe and secure again.

Arriving in San Francisco, Meadow's eyes opened wide, letting in all the sights of this beautiful city: tall buildings, large fountains, the cities inhabitants dressed smartly in the current styles. It was totally surreal for this little girl and beyond her wildest dreams. The two travelers got to Aunt Frances's townhome and were in awe of its grandness and beauty. It was beautiful, with steps up to the front door, and cement columns holding up the large, roofed porch. They had called Aunt Frances when they were an hour away, so she was waiting at the top of the steps for them. Meadow opened her window, and Aunt Frances called out, "There's my favorite nieces! Come up and let me give you hugs." They grabbed their suitcases, ran up the stairs, and their new adventure continued.

Virginia had quit her job at the vegetable packing plant, so they stayed with Frances and Larry for a month. The world was theirs for this brief period, no family interference, just love and happy times. The townhouse was massive: four stories, with a large terrace off the master bedroom that had a circular bed, overlooking the Palace of Fine Arts, a San Francisco landmark to this day. The dining room walls were covered in gold veined mirrors, and music surrounded them, softly coming from ceiling speakers in every room of the home. Aunt Frances loved music, especially the songs of Frank Sinatra, Dean Martin, Johnny Mathis. The music playing made Virginia and Meadow feel like they were in a posh hotel, especially with Aunt Frances's mid-century decorating taste, cream and champagne as the main color scheme. There were touches of silver and deep gold accents as well that made the mother and daughter embrace the feel of San Francisco glamour. Mary could not believe all this, being almost speechless most of the time. She was so happy for her Meadow and wished they could live their forever. "Oh, Meadow, don't you love being here?" Mary excitedly said. Meadow's voice was almost shaky with delight, "Yes, Mary, if only we could."

Aunt Frances took them on tours of the city, in her stylish convertible black Cadillac, El Dorado Biarritz. She bought them clothes and took them to fine restaurants. Aunt Frances would let Meadow and Virginia try on her expensive Fox wraps, along with her diamond necklaces, earrings, and bracelets. They would both parade around the house, gazing at themselves in the tall wardrobe mirrors Aunt Francis had in her dressing closet. It was a huge walk-in closet, storing hundreds of stylish outfits and shoes she wore to all the elegant dinners her and Larry attended as part of the San Francisco elite. It was like a fairytale dream for Virginia and Meadow, a dream neither of them ever wanted to wake up from.

Aunt Frances was aware Meadow knew how to behave out in public: no talking, sit up straight, hands off the table, and speak only when spoken to. These manners were drilled into her brain by Aunt Betty, sometimes with the force of a slap or wire hanging beating. She'd be a good girl, no question. Aunt Frances knew this and reveled in Meadow's grown-up ways at such a young age.

Frances kept the rest of the family updated with weekly calls. She assured them that Virginia and Meadow were safe and enjoying themselves. Their fear of George taking Meadow away had seemed to go away, the two just enjoying their time, feeling safe with Aunt Frances and Uncle Larry. Then Meadow was getting home sick, and it was time to make their way home. They packed up, bid their tearful farewells to Aunt Frances and Uncle Larry, and headed back to reality.

Heading home from their adventure, Virginia had recurring thoughts of George coming and snatching Meadow away to Oklahoma. The hallucinations were more vivid than ever. She could not let him take this last thing away from her. The drive home was quiet, and Meadow was filled with wonderful memories and hope that everything would just be fine. When they got back into town, Virginia stopped at a phone booth and called a man who had befriended her, a local private investigator who genuinely had Virginia's best interests in mind. His name was Seymour, well known and smart about these things. She asked if they could stay with him for a bit, keeping their location secret.

Pete and Janie were also afraid that the alcohol fueled George could come and take Meadow away. He had beaten their daughter, caused all kinds of trouble, and had dropped her off at the ranch without a word to them. They were glad he was out of their lives, and didn't fight this next "secret" location, letting Virginia continue to take over on this part of their safety-from-George journey. It did seem unusual that Pete, Janie, and Betty trusted all this, but talking to Meadow as well, they were convinced it was the safest move before coming home. Meadow was home sick for sure. The falsely instilled fear of her father taking her away seemed to override any trepidation the girl had, so she continued the *secret escape* with her mother.

They stayed at Seymour's for about a month, checking in with Pete, Janie, and Betty every few days to let them know everything was ok, no George in sight. Meadow had to stay inside, never playing outside or being able to stand in the window in case George was sneaking around the outside of the house. She could watch TV, read, or just sit calmly on the couch. She was getting more stressed about this daily life and felt more like a prisoner than a little girl who needed a safe place. Virginia was on her best behavior with Seymour, keeping her emotions and tantrums in check, working the situation to keep them safe from George.

Finally, Virginia felt it was safe to go back to the ranch. This whole trip was mostly a fun excursion for Meadow, with the "secret" traveling, the elegant dining, and feeling protected by Virginia and the others. On the other hand, it was an extremely scary experience thinking she could be kidnapped by George and taken to his family—a family she didn't know and only heard bad things about.

Meadow barely knew her father, and she only saw him a handful of times over the years. Her family had convinced her that George was pure evil, instilling this into her young brain. The few times he did come to town to see Meadow, he had been drinking. This reinforced the only behavior she knew about George and left the girl with a sad feeling in her heart that would never heal. George was just a guy who loved a woman, had a child with her, and drank himself to death at the age of fifty, his liver shot, looking way beyond his years. This is one of those sad tales of a life gone wrong because of alcohol and addictive love.

17

DREAMS BURSTING IN AIR

AFTER THE TRIP TO SAN Francisco, Virginia felt much closer to Meadow. The two were able to bond, spending more time together. She thought, *She's really mine, so we can have fun whenever we want.* Janie was always around to make sure things went smooth between Virginia and Meadow, almost like a watch dog for Betty. Then Betty would come on the weekend, and everything would change. The woman wouldn't give Virginia an inch, continually trying to be the boss over Meadow, never letting Virginia forget how Meadow was safe with the life she had. "That bitch think she knows everything," Virginia would whisper to the bathroom mirror. "Her day will come; that's for fucking sure!"

It was a cool summer, with morning fog drifting away in the afternoon, then returning early evening. This typical summer weather always meant it was cool when the Fourth of July came around, but area fireworks were always a must during this time. The celebration was a magical, fun time, hearing the fireworks for miles around, the sky lighting up with excitement. Janie wouldn't allow fireworks at the ranch as she was fearful something might catch fire. Virginia decided she wanted Meadow to experience fireworks and be up close where there was a huge fireworks display at the beach area some miles north. There were hundreds of people that attended, so getting there early was a must.

With permission from Janie, Virginia said, "Meadow, go take a bath. I'm taking you to see the big fireworks at the beach!" The little girl could hardly speak she was so excited, "Thank you, Mom. I'll get ready." Meadow got her bubble bath ready (she was only five, but she could do this on her own). She slowly stepped into the warm, pink bathtub of water. Excited as she was, Meadow was mesmerized by the warm water and the bubbles. She was envisioning the fireworks in the shiny bubbles, throwing some up with her hand, like dreamy, glistening clouds floating down. She was taking way more time than Virginia wanted her to, and something snapped inside Virginia's mind. She took off her belt from the Levi's jeans she was wearing, and she smacked Meadow in the face saying, "You're taking too long, we need to go!"

Totally shocked, Meadow got out of the tub, her little naked body dripping with water, and she ran to the barn. The barn was not close—about fifty yards away—but she ran the whole way, not caring about getting dirty. Tears were streaming down her cheeks, not understanding what she did wrong. Uncle Raymond was working on a tractor in the yard; her grandparents were visiting friends, so he was the one she could go to. She screamed, "Mom hit me with her belt!" the red welt on her forehead saying it all.

"What?!" Raymond yelled, seeing the little girl was in shock and pain. "I'll take care of this!" He grabbed Meadow in his arms, and they made their way back to the house.

Virginia had gone to the kitchen, smoking her nonfilter Camel. Her head was tilted back, and she inhaled the smoke like it was her last cigarette ever, letting the smoke billow out into the kitchen air. *Now I've done it*, she thought with just a tinge of regret. She smiled that evil smile she would reveal at times when her narcissistic side came out, the complexity of her psychosis bleeding through. Virginia had that defiant look on her face, like no one could get her, no way.

Raymond took off his belt and hit Virginia's right cheek with it, leaving a solid mark. "You'll never hurt Meadow again! See how it feels?!"

Meadow was still crying, not understanding at all. She thought, *Mom never did anything like this; it was always Aunt Betty. Can't I be safe with Mom?*

This was totally out of character for Virginia. She was always on her best behavior around Meadow. She loved her, and the girl was hers, even if she couldn't *legally* take care of her. The built-up anger from who knows where made her snap and take it out on Meadow, with no guilt attached, which was characteristic of her mental state. And yet, no one understood this. To them, it was (again) an example of the craziness of Virginia taking over.

This was the last time anything like this happened between them. The fireworks experience was not happening, so Meadow went to bed with Mary in her arms. Mary wanted to console Meadow, but the girl just wanted to sleep. She was thankful for her savior, Uncle Raymond, and once she drifted off to sleep, she dreamed of glistening clouds that shined like the fireworks she missed. Even though she was young, Meadow still understood that her mom had something wrong with her, that she wasn't totally to blame. Knowing this, Meadow could forgive Virginia. It wasn't her fault. The little girl knew, deep down, her mother loved her.

18

CUTE PIXIE CUT

M EADOW HAD BEAUTIFUL HAIR, SOFT, flowing, medium blonde with just a slight wave to it. It was a rule that her hair had to be washed and ready for styling by whatever day or time that Aunt Betty got home. Betty wanted Meadow's hair to look the way she wanted, as if she was a little statue of a princess to display on a shelf. It was always about presentation and what people would think. "Of course we have to show you off," Betty would say, "People need to see how well we care for you, the little girl who we saved from her awful parents." Time and time again, this was told to Meadow, drilled in her brain so she would never want her parents in her life. But Meadow would never leave Virginia out of her life. Being who she was, she still had love for her, and she was Meadow's confidant whenever she had an "Aunt Betty" problem.

Virginia living at the ranch after the final split with George left the house in town empty. It would have made things way less volatile living at the yellow-and-white house, being separated from Betty, living away from the ranch. But being close to Meadow after all this time and having the support of Pete and Janie was more important, along with the memories of what happened in that house being too painful. Or, maybe, it was to continually to be a thorn in Betty's side.

This was a few months after the San Francisco trip, so the bond between mother and daughter had gotten closer, even with the Fourth of July situation. Virginia would put Meadow's hair into a ponytail every day, her bangs cut short. Virginia was "hands-on" when she could be. Betty was the director of everything Meadow, in charge but rarely showing any true affection with hugging or kisses.

One Saturday, Virginia told Meadow, "Get dressed, we're going into town." "What for?" Meadow asked. "You'll see, it's a surprise!" Virginia replied. Little Meadow went to the bedroom, put on her blouse, denim overalls, socks, and shoes. The little girl was quite capable of doing things herself. In fact, she was determined as ever to *try* to be independent as she could when anyone would let her. The excitement of an adventure with her mom made her tummy tingle. *I'm excited!* she thought, remembering only the fun they had on their road trip.

They got into the Chevy and took off for town. No one was around: the men were working in the fields, and Janie was getting things ready for lunch. Virginia figured the two of them needed some time alone together, still feeling the guilt about losing custody of Meadow, and the Fourth of July occurrence. Deep down, she knew it had been the right decision. Still, the sting of hurt and resentment still lingered in Virginia's being. "Glad Betty's gone somewhere so the two of us can just take off," Virginia mused.

They drove into town, chatting about this and that. Meadow was a smart little thing who could enunciate words well, carry on a conversation. She looked out the window at the fields they passed on their route: alfalfa, lettuce, broccoli growing in neat rows as far as the eye could see. It was so beautiful, and Meadow felt safe. Then Virginia brought up Betty, "Meadow, do you love your Aunt Betty?" Meadow thought for a moment, then replied, "I do." Just to stir up trouble, Virginia said, "Isn't she mean to you? She seems like all she wants to do is tell *you* what to do. Do you think she loves you?" Poor Meadow was put on the spot, the evil part of Virginia coming out to cause trouble. Meadow wondered: *Should I be honest? Will I get in trouble if I am?* Her little voice replied, "Mom, she is mean sometimes, but it's for my own good. I do love her," which was a response she knew would keep her safe. She would learn more of these ways of self-preservation as the years went on. Virginia knew Meadow was trained to respond this way. It had been drilled into her little head repeatedly. "Well, that's fine," Virginia replied. That statement relieved Meadow of any guilt for saying that.

Getting into downtown, Virginia drove them to a little beauty salon that friends of the family owned. They were nice sisters, Mary and Adeline, whose Swiss parents came from the Old Country, part of the Swiss Italian background of Janie and Pete. Meadow questioned, "What are we doing here, Mom?" "You'll see, sweetie," Virginia responded.

Parking, they got out of the truck, Virginia grabbing Meadow's hand as they made their way into the salon. They opened the glass door, calmly strolling inside. Smiling her coy smile, Virginia greeted the ladies: "Hi. How is everyone?" She knew full well that they'd be in shock seeing Meadow with her.

There were four hair-cutting stations, each one back-to-back with round mirrors attached to their workstation. She chose Adeline's station. They slowly walked to the hair styling chair. Meadow climbed up herself, sitting straight as Adeline covered her with the salon cape, the cloth covering the child's body. Adeline slowly asked, "What are we doing today?" Virginia replied, "I want her to have a cute pixie cut, with her bangs shorter, more like my hair. I think she will look darling!" Both sisters were friendlier with Betty and knew all too well the story of the "bad" parents. "Does Betty know you're here?" Adeline hesitantly asked. Seeing Virginia had Meadow alone, she was suspicious as this rarely happened. "It doesn't matter; I'm in charge today!" Virginia replied. Adeline quietly said, "Ok," and went on cutting the girl's hair.

Meadow's excited stomach started to turn into extreme anxiety. She had no idea this was going to happen, her heartbeat increasing by the second. She was so little, barely five, yet so aware of the problem this would cause. Sitting frozen in the chair, Meadow could not move or speak.

Betty had come into town running errands, going to the cleaners, and was getting some new makeup. After all, she deserved new makeup to keep her beauty intact for all to enjoy. She also had a hair appointment at the salon. What's surprising is she had one every Saturday around the same time. Shouldn't Virginia have known that? Or was the timing a coincidence?

Meadow's hair was just finished being cut and styled. It was very cute, but not what she felt comfortable with. She was shocked and scared, thinking, *What would Aunt Betty think? Will I get in trouble? Did Mom do this on purpose?* All these things were running through her precious five-year-old brain.

Betty saw the Chevy in the parking spot and wondered why it was by the salon. *Could Virginia be at a dress store or the drug store?* Betty wondered. Decked out in her stylish weekend clothes, she walked up to the glass door, peered in, and saw Meadow in the salon chair with the new "cut." Betty gasped and rushed in. "What's going on here?!" Betty demanded to know. Adeline was taken aback and said, "Virginia brought Meadow in for a haircut. Isn't it cute?"

Adeline knew then and there that this was a situation she did not want to be part of. Betty replied, "Oh, yes, very cute. Thank you, Adeline," not wanting to seem ungracious by any means. They were all friends socially, almost *like* family. Glaring at Virginia and Meadow, Betty slowly walked past them to Mary's station, smiling at Mary as she sat down.

Meadow was frozen in place like one of those cement yard statues, not being able to move a muscle. She quickly had to release her tiny body as Virginia whispered, "We better go." Virginia paid Adeline, and they made their way out of the salon, through the glass swinging door. Getting into the car, Meadow's shock and fear took over. All the way home there was silence—silence because Virginia was gloating that she'd upset Betty and got *her* way about Meadow's hair, while Meadow couldn't utter a word. Meadow was *her* daughter, and Virginia wanted to control whatever she could, whenever she could. They rode in silence. Meadow hated her hair and was so scared of what would happen to her because of all this. *Why?* Meadow wondered, *Why would Mom do this when she knew what would happen?* Tears started streaming down her little face, trying hard to hold back from sobbing her heart out.

When they got back to the ranch, Meadow got out of the car and ran to the back door. Opening the big door with her little hand, she rushed to her grama, crying and holding onto her for dear life. "Grama, I hate my hair!" her little voice announced. Virginia came in right behind Meadow, revealing, "I only wanted her to look cute. I never meant to cause trouble."

This was a familiar Virginia excuse for everything. Really, Virginia was ecstatic that she got Betty fired up, seeing that hatred in her sister's eyes. *I got Betty this time*, Virginia relished in her mind, saying out loud, "Meadow, you know I love you and only meant to make you happy." Janie did her eyes-wide-open glare at Virginia and told Meadow, "You'll be ok, it will grow back. You do look cute, so don't cry anymore. Go wipe your eyes and wash your hands. Your aunt will be back soon."

And back she was. Betty calmly strolled in with her hair done, makeup in place, looking beautiful. Virginia had escaped to go somewhere while Janie and Meadow were in the kitchen having a snack of cookies and milk, sitting at the end of the long eating table. Betty said quietly, "Meadow, let's go to that small park in town you love so much. Just you and me, for fun. Ok? Go change into that pretty dress I bought you, with the white cardigan sweater. And your black patent-leather shoes."

These were not clothes for the park, by any means. But you never know who you might see that would check out how Betty took care of the girl. It was afternoon and there was still time to enjoy the nice weather outside. Betty's voice sounded so loving that Meadow felt happy, and she really did love that park. Meadow said, "Ok Auntie, I'd love to." Excited, Meadow finished her milk, got changed, and off they went.

The ride there was quiet, not a word said, which made Meadow feel secure. Maybe she wouldn't get in trouble for the haircut? Breathing easy, she just enjoyed the ride and the warm sun shining down. The park was on the west side of the town with a stone building that was used for Boy and Girl Scout troops to meet in. It had a fireplace, so the flagstone stack was visible on the north side of the building, along with the same stone used for the walkway leading to the wooden door. There was a tall hedge around most of the building. It was a privet type, so it was very thick and had been there for a few years. There were spaces between the hedges to walk through, so other kids were running around the spaces, in and out, squealing as they played tag. Next to the building, some feet away, was the jungle gym with swings, a slide, and climbing bars. Meadow was allowed on the swings and slide, but not on the bars. Those were not lady-like, plus she might hurt herself, along with damaging her nice clothes that Betty had worked hard to provide for her.

When they arrived, Betty told Meadow to get out. The aunt went around to Meadow, grabbed her hand, and they walked to the playground. The jungle gym did excite the little girl. She saw other children playing, laughing, and having so much fun that she wanted to be them. Meadow pulled loose from Betty's hand and ran to the hedge, hiding in between the greenery. "Meadow, what are you doing?!" Betty remarked, walking over to where Meadow had hidden. "I hate my hair!" Meadow announced. This was Meadow's way of not taking blame for the haircut, claiming innocence the only way she knew how. "Well, then, you shouldn't have gone with that mother of yours. You know how she is!" Betty said. "I know, Aunt Betty," Meadow replied. "She said we were going for a fun ride, so I thought maybe to this park." Putting the blame on Virginia was the safest thing for Meadow to do…and it was true. Betty said, "Well, it isn't that bad, and it will grow out. We'll make sure this doesn't happen again." Meadow said, "Ok, Aunt Betty."

Now that the haircut confrontation was over, Meadow was relieved and went to enjoy the swings. They stayed for about a half hour, got back into the car, and headed home. As they drove west toward the ranch, the sun was dipping down, barely visible just above the crops, casting a visually warm glow. Meadow felt relieved and content.

Meadow was so happy, thanking her aunt for the outing. Betty replied, "You know I love you, Meadow, and only want the best for you. That's why I'm here, to save your life and be the one to make you happy. Remember, your mother cannot do that for you." True or not, Meadow knew she could have her own feelings about Virginia. Even at such a young age, she understood how her mother was, accepting her quirkiness and enjoying just being around her when she could.

They got out of the car, walking hand in hand into the kitchen. Betty told Meadow to wash her hands, change into her overalls, and she'd be in the bedroom in a few minutes. Meadow did as she was told, and was sitting on the bed when the aunt walked in. Betty had stopped at her parents' bedroom and got the thickest belt she could from her parents' closet. Walking into the bedroom, she told Meadow, "You know I must discipline you for this. We can't have you taking off with your mother like that; there's no telling what might happen!"

Betty told her to undo her overalls, pull her panties down, and lay face down on the bed. She folded the belt and smacked Meadow at least ten times on her butt and legs. Meadow bit her blanket and had tears flowing from her pretty eyes. Betty sternly announced, "Now this will teach you to follow the rules." Betty stopped, turned Meadow around, and said, "Get ready for your bath." Meadow's little body had red welts, and the pain was excruciating.

Janie had heard what was going on and said quietly to Pete, "I knew something would happen to our little girl. We can't let her get in trouble again." Betty helped the girl with her bath, cleaning her well with the washcloth. Meadow was still in shock and just followed whatever Betty told her to do. She then had to go to bed without supper, crying herself to sleep, hugging Mary so tight she almost squeezed the doll's life out of her. Her crying stopped, and the girl drifted off, dreaming of playing at a park in her overalls, getting dirty going down the slide along with the other kids. She noticed the adults looking on and smiling. Their children were having so much fun, and it warmed their hearts that they had this moment in time to share the happiness this play time gave them.

19

KINDERGARTEN FAUX PAS

SOON MEADOW WAS OF SCHOOL age. The girl was smart, articulate, and reveled in the attention she received at home. Kindergarten should be the next educational phase of her life. Meadow had been sheltered living on the ranch, with just her immediate family and working men around her. It seemed enough. Even at this young age, Meadow was able to rebound from anything that Aunt Betty could do to her. She was already building a resistance that wouldn't allow her to succumb to the beatings; she was becoming more outgoing instead of folding inward. The safety of her grandparents continually grounded her, somewhat balancing any negative things that happened.

Virginia decided Meadow was going to kindergarten in the small, coastal village nearby. Most of the students were children of farm workers who came to this country from Mexico for a better life. These were hardworking field workers who were happy to just have a job, sending most of the money they earned back home to Mexico to their less fortunate family. Free schooling was amazing for them: their children could learn things, they were supervised for some hours during the day, and the school was close by.

Meadow was told to get dressed in whatever she wanted because they were going somewhere. "Where are we going, Mom?" Meadow asked with a bit of hesitation in her voice, the hair cut experience still fresh in her mind. Virginia smiled and said, "We're going to see about school for you." In her quiet little voice, Meadow replied, "Does Grama know?" Janie had gone to a doctor's appointment, with Pete driving her. Janie never learned how to drive nor wanted to. With that side look she could do, Virginia quipped, "That doesn't matter. I'm here." They walked outside together, hand in hand with Meadow starting to feel that scared butterfly feeling in her stomach she knew all too well. Getting into the car, Virginia smiled as she said, "It will be fun, you'll see."

The school had no idea Virginia wasn't Meadow's legal guardian. They knew the ranch and the name, so they felt comfortable with any information Virginia gave them. Meadow sat in a chair being quiet as a mouse, knowing not to move or speak. She had been taught well.

When all the information was filled out, the school secretary said, "We'll see you tomorrow, Meadow. We're so happy you're here!" Meadow sank into her chair, not able to respond. Virginia grabbed her hand, and they got into the truck and drove the short trip back to the ranch.

Pete and Janie had gotten home, wondering where the two were. "She knows she shouldn't take off with Meadow!" Janie said out loud. "Please, not another problem!" A few minutes later, mother and daughter strolled in. Meadow was feeling something wasn't quite right. Janie was questioning Virginia about where they had been, and Virginia curtly responded, "It's time Meadow went to school, so I enrolled her in kindergarten. She's smart and needs to be with other kids," knowing full well she only wanted to have some control over Meadow. Her goal was purely selfish and meant to cause trouble, hopefully the most trouble for Betty.

Janie said, "No way is she starting school. She's too young and we want her at home for another year. What's the matter with you? You know you need to ask about these things, Virginia!" Virginia just looked back at her with those squinted eyes, hateful as could be, as she said, "I was only trying to do what was best for *my* daughter, to have her get some education and be smarter than any of us!" Pete just shook his head, letting Janie handle this as usual. "Well, she's not going, and that's that," said Janie. "Now go play, Meadow, and don't worry. You don't have to go to that school." So relieved, Meadow hugged her grama and went off to play in the dirt outside. Virginia got the sternest talking to, fingers pointing at her, and voices raised. Lighting a cigarette, inhaling deeply, and blowing the smoke out with that look of defiance she mastered so well, Virginia said, "Whatever. I was just trying to help."

Meadow's relief was overwhelming. She was just happy she didn't have to go to that school. *My mom was just trying to help*, she assured herself. *She loves me and just wants me to be smart.* This would be true if there wasn't always an underlying agenda to Virginia's motives. For this little girl, justifying her mom's quirky ways kept their relationship congenial and as loving as it possibly could be. Meadow was slowly forming an understanding of the family dynamics: Pete and Janie loved her unconditionally; Virginia loved her but used the girl as an "object" to defy Betty at every turn. And Aunt Betty was the disciplinarian Meadow had to fool as much as possible to keep the beatings at bay.

Grasping this understanding at such a young age allowed Meadow to start forming the tools to mentally deal with the reality of her physical and mental suffering, along with Virginia's unusual behavior at times. This *protection* was her key to survival that grew as she matured. While she couldn't stop Aunt Betty from that determination of discipline the woman thought she had the right to enforce, Meadow could at least build a mental tolerance that got her through these times.

20

THE TIMES, THEY ARE A-CHANGIN'

AS THE YEARS WENT BY, things began to change economically in the dairy and farming business. Larger dairies in Eastern California were consolidating and taking over state milk production. Smaller dairies were becoming a thing of the past, and many (who had land of their own) began growing crops for sale. Pete, Janie, and Raymond only leased the dairy and property, so they had to make some important decisions. It was time for their next chapter.

The collective decision was made to sell off the cows and equipment, making the move into town. Since the house in town was empty, they decided that Pete, Janie, Meadow, and Uncle Raymond would move into it. The house was paid for, the dairy was closed after selling all the ranch equipment and livestock, and living in town was the only choice that made sense. Janie planned on cleaning houses to make extra money, while Pete and Raymond rented land a few miles away to run cattle on, selling them at auction for extra money. Meadow loved the ranch but missed not having close neighbors and other children to play with. She was growing up with a need for more interaction with the world. Being in a neighborhood was scary, but she wanted it so bad. Being six years old and starting first grade, this was the perfect time for their move.

The family of four moved into town, setting the house up, adding ranch home items to the furniture and things that were already in the house. Pete, Janie, and Meadow took over the two bedrooms, while Raymond lived in the third area that could be a dining room or third bedroom. An apartment was rented for Virginia. Janie made sure she had a place to call home, hoping her life would start moving in a positive way. Virginia accepted this and started living her life.

Janie registered Meadow in the local Catholic school, starting first grade. This school (like most other Catholic schools at the time) was very strict, run by the local order of nuns, The Sisters of St. Francis. These women demanded good behavior and ran a very tight, educational ship. This was the early 1960s in a small, conservative, and mostly white town, and the number of Catholic families was quite large.

Being used to a totally different environment, the move to town was a bit of a culture shock for Meadow. Yet once she got there, Meadow started making friends on the block, with her humorous presence that could light up a room. This was the beginning of subtle independence here and there…and Meadow was away from Aunt Betty for time during the day. Little did she realize the nuns would take Aunt Betty's place with the *discipline* section of her life.

When Meadow started at the local Catholic school, Betty made sure she was dressed properly, looking presentable in her uniform. "Make sure you behave today, Meadow. You're lucky you have this opportunity to go to school, and that we're here to take care of you." "Thank you, Aunt Betty. I know I'm a very lucky little girl" was the conditioned answer Meadow knew was the appropriate response, no matter how many times the woman repeated a similar phrase.

Betty would buy clothes *she* wanted Meadow to wear. If Meadow didn't especially like the clothes, she would wear them around Betty but would keep them safe in the closet otherwise. When Betty was going to be at the house, Meadow made sure she had on a nice dress and her black patent leathers with frilly socks. This was the uniform that kept Aunt Betty happy, her little girl looking like the perfect princess. Meadow was uncomfortable in these clothes, so afraid she'd get something on them—a spill of juice, a spot of peanut butter—anything that might set Betty off. The fear was constant, but the rebel in Meadow wanted to think of something to stop Betty in her tracks, get Aunt Betty to understand she wasn't a bad girl, even if she did things that upset her aunt at times. She didn't mean to; she just wanted to get dirty and play like other kids.

Since Betty worked every day, Meadow could wear what she wanted after school and play in the backyard, dirt going wherever she wanted, without fear of yelling or slapping. Pete and Janie knew she needed to play, so they let her enjoy herself in the backyard when she wasn't in school. They would keep her secrets, loving her and understanding the situation. This saved Meadow many times and became a game of looks and winks from Janie when Aunt Betty was around, a game that probably saved Meadow's psyche from going the other way, a way that Virginia had gone.

Betty would return from her job thirty miles away in the early evening to make sure homework would be done, teeth brushed, etc. She'd sleep on the couch as Meadow had her room, the grandparents had their room, Uncle Raymond, his room. Betty didn't mind sleeping on the couch. *I'm making sure everything is going the way it should be raising this girl* she would think. *I'm her savior and she's lucky to have me around.* Betty was sort of a vagabond going from her grandmother Edie's house by work to her parents' house. It seemed like the drive was nothing to her. She drove her car like she was on a racecourse, back and forth, determined to be there for everyone, letting her own life ramble on in uncertainty.

21

GROWING PAINS

Pete and Janie loved and cared for Meadow. Some might say they even spoiled her. And why shouldn't they? She was the bright spot in their lives brought to them by the strife of life occurrences, a gift they never expected at this time of their lives. No matter what happened in Betty or Virginia's lives, they had Meadow they could be proud of and nurture properly.

Betty had a few romantic relationships and went on some dates. The relationships were long term, yet these men finally just gave up as she devoted herself mostly to her family. They were what you'd call "good catches": handsome, fun, good jobs, and they came from quality families. But Betty just couldn't let herself be close enough to them for marriage. Her self-appointed job was to take care of everyone, be selfless, and make sure Meadow behaved.

Betty wasn't much on endearing physical contact. She would reluctantly hug back when greeted, almost like the other person was not worthy of her hug. She didn't enjoy being touched or holding hands, rarely experiencing a kiss (given or received). Sex was not on the menu with any of the men she dated nor anything close to that. It may have seemed that she was following some religious rules or code of ethics and had it in her mind this was her way of being in control as well as her lack of romantic physical attachment. Not even she realized this was the result of her sexual encounter with working man Patrick. That occurrence was seeded deep down in the farthest recesses of her memory bank. It was in a place no one could ever get to.

When Betty would take Meadow to visit Pete's family on the weekend, she'd dress Meadow in a pink dress with a waist tie that went to the back in a bow, frilly sleeves and hem, and those black shiny patent-leather shoes with a strap. Her blonde hair would be clipped on the sides, with bangs that framed her sweet face. When Betty decided Meadow looked just right, they would take off, just the two of them. They'd go to mass first, as the family members were devoted Catholics. After mass, Aunt Betty would stop at the liquor store by the house and make Meadow go in with a quarter to buy the Sunday newspaper. This edition had all the ads with discounts for the next week of groceries, and Janie used as many coupons as she could.

Meadow hated going into the liquor store. The owner scared the girl as his clothes were wrinkled, his fingernails were long and dirty, and he had a creepy half-smile. Her heart would start pounding as they pulled into the parking space. She would hesitate, then Aunt Betty would say, "Now go ahead, don't be afraid!" Meadow would slowly open the door, step out, and meander to the paper stand by the counter. She would give the man the quarter, returning to the car with the newspaper. What may have seemed like a small thing, Meadow's job of getting the paper was a stressful situation for her. Compounded with other things, Meadow would wake up thinking about this task every Sunday morning, seeing the man's smile vividly in her mind. The day would begin with an element of fear.

These Sunday drives were the times that Aunt Betty reinforced all the things she felt Meadow needed to hear. She'd repeat questions trying to find out things about Virginia and the grandparents. Like a police interrogation, Meadow was scared to say the wrong thing. This would make the girl so nervous she wanted to throw up. She thought, *What if I say the wrong thing? I don't want Mom and Grama and Grampa to get in trouble... What should I do?* Telling the truth was easiest. But this is when she realized a small lie here and there wasn't a bad thing to keep things calm—then there would be no yelling when they got back home.

While putting this behavioral pressure on Meadow, Aunt Betty was unknowingly giving her niece the tools to be smarter and stronger in the world, building a resilience that would not let her give in to social pressure or bullying. This took years, but these traits would ultimately thwart Betty at every turn, giving Meadow the ability to psychologically survive. The fact was she had to get through her childhood first before this strength could develop and take hold.

22

ENTICING GLITZ

As one of their Sunday outings, Betty took Meadow to visit Edie, Pete's mom, Meadow's great-grandmother. They called her "Edie Grama," and Betty stayed with her at times to keep her company, as the grandfather, Edward, had died some years ago. With many great-aunts and -uncles and a few cousins living in the town, it was a joyous reunion for Meadow. Even though she was young, she tried to be as good as possible. Meadow would be on her best behavior, trying to keep the peace with Aunt Betty but also wanting to enjoy her time with Edie Grama.

Betty had a bedroom at the house where she kept jewelry, clothes, and personal items. This house was an older farmhouse type in the town, built in the 1920s, with a covered porch, rocking chair and a few plants. Its roofline was gabled on the one side housing a bedroom, with the rest of the roofline being pitched. The inside was a rectangle, having a long hall with the other bedrooms off it. There was a large kitchen, cozy living room, always clean and neat. Meadow just loved Edie Grama and so looked forward to these overnight outings.

Betty was now driving a two-door black Chevy Impala, sleek and cool, with dark-orange leather interior. She really felt like Liz Taylor, cruising around town in the upscale car. While Betty didn't seem to *ask* for attention, she sure relished being stared at when she drove the vehicle, especially when the men yelled "Hey, honey!" and whistled, filling her ego to the brim. It was a great traveling car that Meadow also enjoyed driving back and forth in.

Pulling up to the house. Aunt Betty warned Meadow, "Remember to be good. Edie Grama won't put up with any bad behavior." Betty's voice was stern yet not too loud, a typical volume when she knew others were around. Meadow grabbed her small suitcase and followed the aunt in. The flowers growing in the yard were colorful and caught her eye, causing her to slip on one of the porch steps. "Meadow!" whispered the aunt, "Watch your step!" Meadow raised herself up, a bit shaken from the experience. "I'm sorry, Aunt Betty, I'll be better…" Meadow said.

They settled inside, greeting and hugging Edie. There was a snack of cookies and milk waiting for Meadow, coffee for Betty. After putting her things neatly in the bureau drawer (as she was well taught), Meadow wandered to the kitchen for her treat. After they finished their snack and chatted for a bit, Betty said she had to run some errands. A relief came over the little girl, looking forward to spending alone time with her safe great-grandmother. Edie was a gentle soul who had raised six children, yet she wasn't worn out from life. Every day she wore a nice dress with a beautiful broach on her left lapel, along with quality shoes. Her gray hair was always well styled, and she was a pleasant person to be around. Edie was loved by everyone, especially her family, who had great respect for her as the matriarch of the family. Aunt Frances made sure her mother was well taken care of financially, along with showering her with lots of clothes and jewelry.

Betty had a jewelry box in her part-time bedroom. Why she enjoyed living like a vagabond was beyond everyone's thinking. The family just accepted this believing it was because she wanted to help everyone so much. It took her away, so she didn't have time to think about her shortcomings, which were unnecessarily manifested in her own mind. A constant *I'm not good enough, we're poor* feeling was embedded into Betty's brain. She despised wealthy people and their "better than you" perceived attitude. Yet, she also embraced them to be part of their lives and circle. None of it made sense.

The jewelry box had lovely trinkets tucked away that were accessible at any time. For not wanting to seem wealthy, Betty had beautiful jewelry she wore daily, many pieces being gifts from employers and male friends. Meadow's interest in this box was piqued by the fact that she was told not to go near it. After the snack, they went into the living room to sit on the couch. Meadow's inquisitive personality got the best of her, so she told Grama Edie she had to go into the bedroom for something. "Ok, baby. Just don't mess up your aunt's things. You know how she is." The girl immediately went into the room, looked around, and saw a small chair in the corner. She dragged it over to the dresser so she could stand up on it to view the forbidden "fruit" on the top of the dresser. The jewelry box was one of those taller ones (a bit like a small dresser), with a top that opened and a few drawers down the front being constructed of beautiful maple wood. While Meadow was shaking a bit from fear, she went ahead and started taking out jewelry. She was a magnet for jewelry, loving the beauty of the chains and the shimmering jewels. She knew this was wrong but just couldn't help herself. There were beautiful bracelets, dangling earrings, long necklaces, rings galore…a super treasure of goodies to try on!

To the left was a wardrobe mirror laying against the closet door. Meadow put on the jewelry along with a hat her aunt had sitting on the dresser. She tried on lots of bracelets with various stones, gold and silver chains, the necklaces falling around her neck down to her tiny waist. She got down from the chair and walked slowly over to the mirror, not disturbing any of the adornments on her small frame. "Oh, I look so beautiful," she softly said. "I'm pretty!" She paraded around the bedroom a bit, hearing the jewelry sing its jingling songs. Edie Grama heard Meadow's voice, walked down the hall to the bedroom, came in and said, "Sweety, you better put that jewelry away now, you know how your aunt is. And make sure everything is put away just like you found it."

Edie was aware of Betty's input into Meadow's life, as were all the members of the family. They all appreciated Betty taking care of Meadow, saving her. Thankful, yes, but they were also aware of how the other side of Betty can come out at times—especially with Meadow. "I will, Edie Grama," Meadow responded in her soft, little voice. She took all the jewelry off and tried to remember where each piece went, going as quickly as possible.

Edie and Meadow were sitting on the couch just chatting about nothing, both giggling a bit, when Betty came through the door carrying bags of food and a few clothes she had just purchased. She was always charging things on credit cards with the purest of intentions to pay them off each month. But—and a *big* but—she always had to ask her parents for extra money to get her out of financial jams. It wasn't that she meant for this to happen; she just needed to look nice and represent the family well with her current fashions. They didn't mind… After all, she was helping with their Meadow.

Betty took her items into the bedroom, placed them on the bed, and screamed in shock. Meadow had left one necklace dangling out of a drawer of the jewelry box, and one earring had fallen to the floor. Racing out of the room, Betty grabbed Meadow off the couch, threw her face down on the bed, pulled down her small pants, showing her bare butt. Edie was shocked but stayed on the couch. She would never interfere with Betty's discipline of Meadow.

Betty went to the closet, took out a wire hanger, bent it in half, and started smacking her rear repeatedly with the hanger, yelling, "Didn't I tell you not to get into my things, especially my jewelry!? You need to learn not to touch other people's things!" Betty gave Meadow repeated swats with the hanger, fiercely saying those same words each time. Meadow's poor butt was red and bleeding, the pain going through her body as the hook had caught her skin and made a deep scratch. The girl was frozen, screaming and crying uncontrollably. Edie came in and said (politely), "You better stop that now. She understands," and Betty finally stopped.

Meadow just laid there as Betty cleaned the hanger and hung it back in the closet. It was as if the whole world had stopped, creating a situation that was never forgotten. It was an experience that stayed in Meadow's brain for a lifetime, as vivid as the day it happened. Edie Grama cleaned Meadow up, then held her until she stopped crying, and saying, "It's ok, she loves you and only wants the best for you."

Just like the rest of the family, they only saw that Meadow had been saved from drunken, crazy parents and was so lucky to have a family that loved her. The abuse was thought of as discipline, and they viewed it as just Betty's way of helping get Meadow raised well with good standards. Little did they know the deep scars that came with all that discipline would last a lifetime.

The day went on as if nothing had happened. They ate dinner with Edie Grama and shared small talk about relatives, the weather, and things of no consequence. Meadow ate quietly, trying to be as good as possible not to upset Aunt Betty, no dropping food on her dress or spilling milk on Edie Grama's beautiful, embroidered tablecloth.

When it was time for bed, Meadow got undressed, neatly hanging up her dress on one of the wire hangers she knew all too well, then quietly took off her shoes, placing her socks inside of them. She removed her neatly folded pajamas from the dresser drawer, the dresser where the jewelry box hid the beautiful jewels that had been enticing to Meadow.

After making sure her pajama buttons were in place and that her bottoms were pulled up properly, she climbed up onto the soft mattresses happy that the day was over. Aunt Betty tucked her in, kissed her on the forehead, and said, "You know I do love you and only want the best for you?" Meadow softly replied, "I know, Aunt Betty, I love you too." The little girl was too scared to say anything different, finally realizing it was the smartest sentence she could say to the woman.

23

AIN'T NUN O' DAT

T HE SUNDAY VISIT TO GRAMA Edie's was a thing of the past once Monday rolled around. They got up early to bring Meadow home as Aunt Betty had to go right back to get to work, her maniac driving as usual. Meadow was still sore from the hanger episode, the scratch already starting to heal. Learning to be resilient from these episodes and having Mary when she got home to talk to, Meadow was happy that Monday meant school and seeing all her new friends. Once she got used to going to school and being around all those kids, her personality started to blossom, and she was able to forget about Aunt Betty's rules. She became more outgoing and gregarious than the others, most of them gravitating toward her, almost living vicariously through Meadow. It was as if these children wanted to be like her but just couldn't let their fear of getting in trouble allow them the fun she seemed to have. This got her in hot water many times until she understood what was going on. She had learned that with Aunt Betty, she had to tell a fib sometimes to save herself from a slap. *This should work the same at school, right?* she'd think. Let's just say the nuns were way smarter than Betty and onto the girl's games.

One day Meadow's classmates dared her to lift Sister Roberta's veil to see if she had hair trailing down her back. These were the days when the nuns wore full caps with veils, long sleeves, flowing dresses, and rosary beads around the waist. The habits were all black and made from a quality cotton/nylon fabric so they would last for years, teaching the nuns to be thrifty. Of course, Meadow took on the challenge.

While the class kept Sister Roberta busy with questions, Meadow snuck out of her small, wooden desk, crept around the right side of the class-room, and went behind the nun. She thought, *Boy, have I fooled her*, be-lieving Sister Roberta hadn't noticed her at all. Meadow slowly lifted the veil up as high as she could when the sister turned around and gave her a *slap! Bam!* Meadow was shocked and fell back against the chalkboard, the pain of the previous day's Aunt Betty incident more evident when she fell. She let out a soft "ow" that hardly anyone heard.

The class was giggling, trying to hold back their laughter, until Sister Roberta reeled around and yelled, "Stop that now!" Everyone just froze. Meadow was yanked to the principal's office where she was scolded and wrapped on the knuckles with a ruler, something that was done without recourse during these times, just accepted as permissible "nun" behavior. "You must learn to respect us, Meadow! Remember how lucky you are to be here *and* to have your grandparents raise you! No more of these she-nanigans!" Sister Marian told Meadow to go back to class, where everyone was still in shock about what had happened.

Meadow had no idea if they would tell her family, so she just kept it quiet, not breathing a word about it after she got home. Janie asked how school was, and Meadow responded, "I had a nice day," just hoping she wouldn't get in more trouble. Fortunately, it was kept at school, so the young girl had a moment of relief. No repercussions from Aunt Betty, no fear of another beating. She needed to realize that authority figures had to be minded.

What continued to come from these events was a stronger person, learn-ing to withstand more to survive. While Meadow would always test the waters, she made sure she kept on the good side of the Catholic Nuns that seemed to have as much control over her life as Aunt Betty. But that control was only for a few hours a day whereas Aunt Betty's control might never go away. The raps on the knuckles were a far cry from Aunt Betty's wire hanger beatings.

24

BALLERINA DREAMS

L IKE AT EDIE GRAMA'S, BETTY kept a dresser at Pete and Janie's house for when she stayed over. It was filled with underwear, nylons, jewelry, and anything else she could shove in there. She wasn't the neatest person, so things would hang out, almost falling off the edge of the drawer. Janie washed any clothes Betty left around, folding them or hanging them neatly, and often organized the drawers for when Betty came back. Janie was happy to do this as Betty was a hard worker and helped with the family so much that she didn't have time to keep things neat and tidy.

For some reason, these drawers intrigued Meadow. Knowing the consequences after the incident at Edie Grama's, the fascination she had with the sparkling jewelry, statues, and music boxes on top of the dresser would get the best of this little girl. Now seven, the *jewelry* memory at Edie Grama's was distant and she pushed it aside. Her inquisitive and challenging nature took over one more time.

This was a simple, old oak dresser, the kind that had curved drawers and an oval mirror attached to two wood pieces that came up from the back of the dresser. You could move the mirror back and forth, depending on the size of the person using it. In this case, the mirror faced downward, as Betty was a short person, which she resented her whole life. Being angry when someone mentioned her size, she'd later report, "I can do twice the work they can!"

Although she wasn't the neatest person, Betty had the top items organized in a certain way. She had changed things up in the drawers as well, putting underwear in a different place along with bras. Unusual for her, Betty had folded them neatly, thinking she'd help with her mom's constant workload.

Meadow had been thinking about those drawers and top goodies, knowing not to touch them as she was constantly warned. When Meadow got home from school, she changed out of her uniform and put on some comfortable clothes that Aunt Betty had approved. She kept thinking about that dresser, not being able to resist the temptation. As always, Janie had milk and cookies waiting for her. Meadow ate them, gulped down the milk, and took off toward the bedroom. The dresser was calling.

Meadow got a chair from the adjacent dining room, climbed up, and started looking at all the goodies on the dresser. She knew Aunt Betty hated her not following orders, but it was something she just had to do, to test and see that maybe this time it would be ok. And she was older now and more careful, she was sure of that. *I am seven now, so I'm way smarter than when I was little*, she thought.

She checked everything out, opening the music boxes and watching the ballerina dance in circles. The ballerina mesmerized Meadow. Her mind drifted for a minute, thinking how being a ballerina could be something she'd have talent for. Mary was close by and agreed, "You'd be a beautiful ballerina, Meadow. I can see you in the toe shoes and one of those tutus gliding around the dance floor." Meadow nodded in agreement. Then her mind heard Aunt Betty's voice: *"You could never be a ballerina. You're way too clumsy and not thinly built like* those *girls."*

That inner voice brought Meadow back to the task at hand. The small China box with the rose embossed on it was so beautiful that she kept opening it. Nothing was inside, but it was so pretty and played a beautiful song on its own. Meadow stopped and opened the top drawer of the dresser, looking everything over with her wandering eyes. She pulled out a bra, tried it on, and looked at herself in the mirror. "One day, I'll wear one of these and be a grown-up too," she said using her best grown-up voice.

Meadow heard Janie coming down the hall, so she quickly put the bra back and tried to arrange everything just like it was. Meadow got off the chair, and said, "Grama, I was just looking, not touching." "Good, honey. You know how Aunt Betty is about her things. Let's put the chair back and help me with the potatoes," Janie replied. Meadow hated peeling potatoes and the girl was terrible at it. But Janie wanted to take up Meadow's time and have her learn more about cooking.

Pete and Raymond hadn't gotten back from the ranch that they leased to run cattle. This was profitable for them, but mostly it was something for them to do every day, giving them purpose. After closing the dairy, they needed something to take them to the country where they had peace and quiet, away from the confines of small houses. Raymond had ultimately bought his own home a few miles away and enjoyed the solitude it gave him.

Meadow was helping Janie in the kitchen when Betty got home. As usual, Betty was exhausted from the bookkeeping job she had, cranky and snapping back like she was the only person in the world who had had a busy day at their job. The stage was set for something to go wrong; Meadow felt it. And so did Mary.

Betty walked into the bedroom, threw her purse on the bed, and kicked off her shoes. She wanted to look as professional as possible, so she wore high heels that were in style, appealing more to the men than anyone else in the office. They looked good, and she got tons of compliments. But at the end of the day, her feet were so tired she could hardly wait to take those shoes off. Too tired to take a bath, she took off her clothes, underwear, and bra and went over to her dresser. She looked at the things on top, noticing they were all moved around in the wrong places. She had specifically put the ballerina music box to the left for ease of opening, and it was way on the right, up at the corner of the dresser. "What the heck?!" Betty blurted out.

Then Betty saw a bra strap hanging out of the drawer, knowing she had neatly placed things in the drawer, and that Mama would never let that hang out like that. She quickly put on her robe and yelled, "Meadow!" Meadow was still fiddling around with the potatoes. When she heard

Aunt Betty's voice, her eyes opened so wide they almost popped out of her head. Her heart sank, her stomach got butterflies, and terror ran through the rest of her body. *How did she know I had been in her dresser?* her young mind thought.

Meadow slowly got up from her chair at the yellow kitchen table, the Formica top covered in potato peels. Janie darted her a look, throwing her a towel she could wipe her shaking hands with. She whispered, "Didn't I tell you to leave that dresser alone? You know how she is!" without a thought of protecting the girl or going against Betty.

Meadow dragged herself into the bedroom, wondering what pain this punishment would bring, tears already streaming down her cheeks. Betty was fierce with anger. Her day had been crazy and all she wanted to do was change clothes and relax. "Don't you understand how hard I work to help you?! My day was awful and now you touch my things!! Why would you do that?" "I don't know Aunt Betty. I just love your things. I won't do it again," Meadow quietly replied. "Oh, I'm sure you won't, little girl. Come here," Betty said as she motioned for Meadow to come over to her.

Betty was in front of the dresser looking over things. The top drawer was opened where the bra strap was hanging out. She picked Meadow up, put her little right hand over the drawer, and slammed it shut on the girl's tiny fingers. Meadow screamed the highest pitch you could imagine, and blood started streaming down from her fingers. The pain was as much as being smacked with a wire hanger, only it was more concentrated on her fingers. She was sobbing as Betty opened the drawer up. "Now look, you got blood on my bra!" yelled Betty. "Now go wash your hands and I'll come in a put a bandage on the boo-boo. You know I don't enjoy hurting you, honey, but you need to learn to do what I say."

Betty said this in a way that sounded as if the woman wasn't at all phased by the act, that hurting the girl was just part of her daily routine and to-tally acceptable by any standard. Betty just couldn't (or wouldn't) control that part of herself—the part that challenged her to have total power over Meadow. It was a power that was relentless yet unforgivable on any level.

Janie ran in, grabbed Meadow, and took her to the bathroom. "I'll take care of it," Janie said, giving Betty the sternest look she could, her pink cheeks redder than ever. Janie held Meadow in her arms to comfort her for a minute. Then Janie put Meadow's hand under the cold water to stop the bleeding. Fortunately, only one finger had a cut, a Band-Aid taking care of stopping any further blood. "Honey," said Janie said, "we need to be very careful and follow what Aunt Betty tells us. She loves you and only wants you to be a good girl and behave properly."

By the time everything had calmed down, Pete and Raymond had gotten home from the cattle ranch, famished and ready for a "Janie" feast. Everything seemed fine. Dinner was almost on the table, glasses set with water, wine, and milk. When Pete questioned Meadow about her bandaged finger, she softly said, "I hurt it playing in the orchard with a branch." Pete responded, "You need to be careful, young lady. Fallen branches are very dangerous." Janie sternly glanced over at Betty as she was agreeing with Pete. "Yes, Papa, she needs to be careful, those branches can hurt her badly."

Pete felt like it was a good day. The cattle were fattening up, and the summer sun was setting with its glow of light spreading across the sky before the coastal fog bank rolled in and cooled things off. He had such a nice family. It was a blessing to enter the house where everyone was calm and quiet.

When it was time for bed, Aunt Betty tucked Meadow in, giving her a kiss on the forehead. She repeated the usual conversation trying to make up for hurting the girl, the same as George would do with Virginia after a drunken beating. In her nicest voice possible, she softly whispered, "I love you, Meadow. I just want you to be the good girl I'm proud of." Meadow meekly replied "I know Aunt Betty. I love you too."

When Meadow finally fell asleep, she had dreams of being the ballerina in the music box, floating, twirling, jumping, and gracefully landing on her spot in the box. The tinkling melody played, while she heard soft applause from the audience praising her performance. Then Aunt Betty slammed the box shut, turning the dream into a nightmare of reality, abruptly waking up. She was holding on to her Mary so tight she thought she'd squeeze the life out of her little friend.

25

PERFORMANCE SINS

DURING MEADOW'S YOUNGER SCHOOL YEARS, after work Betty would drive the half hour back to Meadow's house to make sure she got her homework done. While she didn't have that much knowledge about math or other subjects, Betty was determined to make sure Meadow got her work done on time with correct answers. She'd grill the girl, expecting perfect answers on all the subjects. Meadow was smart, but not necessarily great in certain areas. About an hour before Betty would arrive, Janie would warn Meadow, "She'll be here soon, so you better have that homework done."

That threat was like putting an arrow through Meadow's little heart. She'd make sure to get the work done in time, her heart pounding. When Aunt Betty arrived, she'd go right to the kitchen table where Meadow was working, warn her it better be done and correct, and then she would look things over. If the homework wasn't up to Betty's standards, Meadow would be taken to her room for a stern talking to. "I need to make sure you are raised right and get good grades for your future" was the repeated mantra. There wasn't physical abuse regarding the homework being done or correct, just Betty's raised voice and threats that added to an already stressful environment.

Reports cards were the worst stressor for Meadow. She wasn't the best at school, but she got decent grades, mostly Bs and Cs. She tried hard wanting to please Aunt Betty to keep the peace at home. Betty would circle the dates that report cards were being given out. She used her checkbook calendar for this, looking to see when to ask about the report card just in case Meadow forgot to tell her they had been given out. The lady was like a detective about these things, being a sleuth who no one was going to get the best of. *Nothing* could get past her.

The first report card of the year was the hardest for Meadow. Summer was over, and students had to get their brains wrapped around studying rather than playing. And the threat of Christmas presents being taken away was so scary. "Santa will know if you got bad grades so you better be a good girl or no presents!" was always the threat. Aunt Betty would keep this mantra up during the whole fall semester, a constant threat that weighed so heavy on Meadow she sometimes would have dreams of Santa quickly flying past her house.

Report cards came just before Thanksgiving break. The nun Meadow had as a teacher called everyone up to her desk one by one to hand them the report card as they were leaving the classroom for the break. She gave Meadow a stern look and said, "Have a nice Thanksgiving holiday. Please try harder next time." This set up Meadow's anxiety-driven reality as she left the classroom. Before opening the envelope, Meadow took a deep breath, thinking, *Please let these be good grades*, even though she had been prewarned.

Slowly tearing the flap open, Meadow slid the report card from the small manila envelope. As the reality of what she saw registered in her brain, her heart started pounding, her breathing becoming faster and faster. To her alarm, there was only one B, and the rest were C's. She knew this wasn't a good thing and was scared to death of the consequences.

On the ride home with the neighbor who had three girls at the school (Janie didn't drive so she gave the neighbor gas money for driving Meadow back and forth to school), she kept trying to think of ways to hold off sharing this with Aunt Betty. Meadow brainstormed, *Can I say I forgot it at school?* or *The Sister forgot to hand them out.* Her head was spinning to try and think of an excuse that would save her from the pain of Aunt Betty's wrath. Nothing seemed like it could work. Meadow would just have to face the music or come up with a plan at the last minute.

Aunt Betty came to the house for the holiday weekend. She was exhausted as usual and was complaining about work and the lazy people she worked with. "Can't anyone carry their load?! Do I have to do everything?" This was her constant complaint. She would say this repeatedly during her work life—Betty wondered aloud why no one had the work ethic she had, why they were so lazy, and why they weren't raised right.

For some reason this time, Betty didn't remember about the report cards. Maybe from being tired. Or maybe just because it wasn't a priority at the time. Meadow kept waiting to be asked about the report card. That wouldn't happen till the Friday after Thanksgiving.

Meadow was on her best behavior for Thanksgiving dinner. It was held at Edie Grama's house with all the relatives there. Virginia was her obstinate self and wouldn't attend the festivities, being the victim of some ailment or such. Everyone asked where Virginia was, and Betty thought, *That's Virginia, always trying to be the center of attention, even by not being with us!* The dinner was fun; everyone laughed, drank wine, and made memories with family that Meadow loved—and who loved her back just as much.

Friday came, and Meadow knew the report card would come up but seemed to forget all about it. The weather was warm, which was not unusual for fall on this California coast. Meadow went down to play on the next block. Living alone with adults for so many years, it was a blessing to interact with children her age, and she loved every minute of it. The group played for a few hours—hide-and-seek, running races, and hopscotch. They were all so excited to have a break from school, feeling free during these moments in time. The sun was falling behind the row of houses on the west side of the street, so it would be dark out soon. Meadow hadn't remembered about the report card while she was playing, but then she heard a stern voice approach. "Meadow, I need you to come with me." That serious Aunt Betty voice meant she was in trouble, and Meadow's heart started to pound.

Meadow had hidden her report card in her sock drawer. Aunt Betty never went into those drawers—only Janie and Meadow. Grama Janie was the one who washed, dried, and put things away for her granddaughter, as she did for Betty. It was something Janie loved to do, was trained to do, and did it to be useful to Meadow, to show her love. Betty had looked at her checkbook calendar to see when the report card should show up. Checking the date, she knew it was there somewhere.

Betty questioned Janie who hadn't thought about it and had no idea where it was. Pete wasn't back from the hills yet. He was of no use about these things anyway. *Hmmmm*, Betty thought. *Now, where would this little girl have put her report card?* She hoped Meadow wasn't hiding it or trying not to show it to her. Or maybe she had forgotten it at school. That would be enough to reprimand her on its own, not paying attention to her responsibilities. Betty wondered, *Would she be that stupid, like that mother of hers?*

Looking around the bedroom, Betty checked under the bed and mattress, investigated the closet, checking all the pockets in clothes and coats. Nothing there. "Maybe her dresser?" Betty said out loud. She started rummaging through Meadow's drawers, moving things all around. She was really hoping her niece had forgotten the report card at school. Finally, she saw the manila envelope with Meadow's name on it. Aunt Betty's eyes opened wide, anger coursing through her body, "That little bitch! She hid this from me!! What's the matter with her?!" Those words could not depict the true rage she felt. Then Betty opened the envelope, taking the card out. That did it. Those grades told her what a lazy girl Meadow was. Betty would teach her a lesson. Lessons that she knew were turning her into a quality person, unlike those parents who bore her.

There was silence on the way to the house. Aunt Betty held Meadow's hand tightly, guiding her on the sidewalk if Meadow lagged at all. The sun had just set when they walked into the house, lights in the house on and glowing. Janie was involved in cooking dinner, potatoes boiling on the stove, and the roast almost done in the oven. Meadow loved the smell of Grama Janie's cooking. It always made her feel safe and loved.

Betty pulled Meadow into the bedroom and slammed the door shut. Janie looked up from her cooking, wondering why the door closed, but figured it was just them coming home from down the block. It didn't occur to Janie there was a storm brewing in that bedroom. Aunt Betty showed Meadow the report card and asked, "Why such bad grades, Meadow? I coach you every night with your homework, making sure you do it right. Don't you pay attention in class, or are you too busy being the class clown? Nobody likes a showoff girl!" Meadow's insides were a mess. The only answer she could come up with was, "I don't know, Aunt Betty. I try hard and pay attention in class." "Are you just stupid like your mother then? And why did you hide that report card from me?" Aunt Betty responded. "I didn't, Aunt Betty. I just forgot to show you," Meadow replied. They both knew that was a lie, but it was the only thing the girl could come up with.

"What are we going to do with you? You have all these chances most little girls don't have and you throw them away! The only thing left to do is remind you to do better next time," Betty said, which meant that a hanger whipping was in store. "Yes, Aunt Betty," Meadow weakly replied. "I'll do better, I promise." Knowing what was in store, Meadow's body sank, and her mind started drifting away.

Betty told her to bend over the bed, her face on the bedspread. Betty grabbed a hanger from the closet, folding it to fit the girl's body better, to inflict more pain. She pulled Meadow's pants down and swatted her repeatedly. Meadow kept saying, "I'll do better, Aunt Betty, I promise," the tears she tried to hold back were streaming down her cheeks.

Finally, it stopped. This time only red welts were evident. Aunt Betty pulled Meadow's pants up, turned her around, kissed her forehead, and said, "You know I love you, honey. I only want the best for you. This is over and we'll work harder for better grades, ok? Lesson learned?" Meadow softly said (between tears), "Yes, Aunt Betty. I know you love me. Without you, I would be on the street starving, or dead. My grades will get better, and I will pay more attention in class." Betty wiped Meadow's tears away and fixed the little girl's ponytail. Betty took her to the mirror and said, "You look good. Now let's go eat!"

The table was set, and dinner was ready. Pete had just gotten home from the hills. He went to the sink, washed his hands, thinking how hungry he was and how the aroma of Janie's cooking always made him feel better. Betty and Meadow walked into the kitchen and sat down at their places, Meadow kissing Pete on the cheek. "I love you, Grandpa. Thank you for taking care of me." Janie served the food. Everyone ate, chatting about their day, no mention of the heinous act that had occurred in Meadow's bedroom. The fall moon was coming up and you could see it through the kitchen window, its glowing light giving hope for a new day this family wanted and deserved.

26

LAND OF DISNEY'S DREAMS

WALT DISNEY'S DREAM OF CREATING a wonderland utopia opened on July 17, 1955. Visiting Disneyland was every child's dream; a "greater-than-life" dream that was fueled by Disney's Sunday TV evening show *The Magical World of Disney*. For someone like Meadow, that dream never seemed like it could become a reality. She didn't come from a rich family, and she knew that a trip like that would cost a good deal of money. It was a pipe dream, but a dream for the girl, nonetheless.

It was the last semester of fourth grade, and Meadow's report card was the best yet: two As and the rest were Bs. Even though she knew these grades were good, would they be good enough for Aunt Betty? Her doll mate, Mary, didn't think so. "My Meadow, you know your grades will never be good enough for that witch!" she whispered. "We have to protect you no matter what." "Oh, Mary, I think this time you might be wrong," Meadow replied. Mary was rarely wrong, but this time Meadow hoped she was. The doll just stared at the girl with that look of doubt she had sometimes. She was still smiling, so Meadow felt this was a good sign.

The time came to show Aunt Betty the report card. "Very good," Betty said. "I knew you would end up smarter than that mother of yours." Meadow beamed with confidence and a big smile. "Thank you, Aunt Betty, I tried really hard!"

The next week was uneventful, the school year finishing on Thursday of that week. All the kids were happy, giddy, and ready for a nice summer.

The next day, Meadow was playing in the backyard, wearing overalls and tennis shoes, the afternoon sun being a bit clouded by some fog. Mary was by her side helping Meadow to have a fun time. Betty had gotten off work early to come by the house. She walked in, said hello to Janie in the kitchen, and asked where Meadow was. Janie was doing her usual precooking of things for dinner and responded, "She's playing in the backyard."

Janie knew what was going on and almost couldn't contain her excitement. Janie was sometimes like a child herself, which always had been part of her charm.

Betty walked out into the yard. When she saw Meadow, Betty said, "Meadow, I want you to go get changed. We're going on a little trip." "Ok, Aunt Betty," was all she could say. *What is going on? Where is she taking me? Am I in trouble?* These thoughts quickly raced across Meadow's brain.

Meadow brushed off any dirt that had gotten on her clothes, grabbed Mary, and started heading into the house. Stopping, Meadow turned around and asked, "What should I wear?" hoping to get an idea of where they were going. "Put on your nicest dress, with your black patent-leather shoes, the slip-ons with the ribbon ties. Don't forget your new socks with the ruffled edges I bought you. I want you to look your most beautiful!" Betty excitedly replied.

On her way through the kitchen, Meadow looked over at Grama Janie and got the most pronounced wink she had ever seen Janie give, along with her rosiest Mrs. Claus cheeks. This made Meadow more excited than ever.

Betty told her to also pack her little suitcase with things for an overnight stay for where they were going. This peaked Meadow's interest even more. "See Mary, I told you I would get rewarded for my good grades," Meadow said to the doll. "You know that Aunt Betty does love me!" Mary replied, "Just beware of this lady. You know how she can get if you say the wrong things or forget your manners. I won't be there to help!" Meadow responded, "Ok Mary, I'll try to remember that." The girl's heart was racing with excitement about the prospect of going somewhere. She'd behave and be a good girl for sure.

"Time to go, Meadow," directed Aunt Betty. "We have a long drive ahead of us." Meadow obeyed, kissed and hugged Grama Janie who whispered "Have a good time. I love you Meadow." She took her suitcase out to the car, placed it gently on the back seat, and slid into the passenger side of the car. The excited girl knew to sit quietly while she waited for her aunt. Betty got in, started the car, and off they went. They drove to the freeway and headed south, driving in Betty's cool Chevy two-door, Meadow loving the car and the adventure ahead. It was about a four-hour drive to Anaheim, where Disneyland was, and the speed (at this time) was dictated by the safety of the conditions on the road (weather, etc.) Betty was almost like a race car driver when her foot hit the petal. The fact that she drove daily to and from work on the northern part of the freeway, the woman had become fearless driving at higher speeds, never getting a speeding ticket or into an accident. This gave her the confidence to drive any speed she wanted, regardless of the weather conditions.

There was still no mention of where they were going. Meadow knew she couldn't ask, or she would get yelled at, slapped, or something worse. She kept her mouth shut, determined not to let Mary win this time. With Betty's driving being a bit uneven, Meadow started to get pains in her stomach, feeling nauseous from the drive. Suddenly, Meadow yelled, "I'm going to throw up, Aunt Betty!" They were driving along the ocean and Betty had time to pull over and stop along the road. Meadow opened the door and let any food she had in her stomach burst out, spraying some on the inside of the door. Betty grabbed a towel from the trunk, threw it at Meadow, and said, "Clean up your mess!"

Betty was livid that this had happened, letting it almost ruin the trip. Meadow was a bit shaken but managed to clean her mouth and the door. She got back into the car, and they took off on the freeway. Betty was beside herself and yelled, "What's the matter with you?! Why did this happen?!" "I don't know," Meadow meekly answered. This had never happened to her, and she wasn't sure why she threw up. It was Betty's swerved driving that caused the girl's car sickness. and if Mary had been there, she'd say it for sure. Not a word was spoken till they made their next stop.

They traveled on until they got to Du-Pars, the famous restaurant just north of Los Angeles. Aunt Betty cautioned Meadow and stated, "Now we're going to eat at this nice restaurant. Please behave!" They pulled into the parking lot and Meadow's eyes opened wide. She rarely got to go to a restaurant, and this was the nicest she had ever been to. They walked through the glass doors and were greeted by the friendly hostess who took them to their booth with the leather tufted, brown toned seating. Meadow didn't ask what she could get, because she figured it was safer to let Aunt Betty order. To her surprise, Betty let Meadow order for herself. So, Meadow made sure she ordered something a nice little girl would order: a small hamburger, mashed potatoes, and just water to drink. She felt this was safe and wouldn't get a slap from this choice of food.

Aunt Betty ordered her food too. The food came out quickly. They ate slowly, as Meadow was taught. "Don't eat like you're starving, like we never feed you!" as she would say to Meadow at the kitchen table. Meadow was also eating slower as her stomach hadn't fully recovered from the *throwing up* episode. Looking around at the different people who were in the restaurant, Meadow was intrigued by how nice everyone was dressed. They were having cocktails along with their food, most of them smoking while they ate, yacking about this and that. Meadow couldn't wait to tell Mary about this!

Finishing their meals, Betty paid, and they got back into the Chevy. The car quickly made it to the freeway entrance, and off their journey continued. Meadow was just hoping they'd get to where they were going so she could just relax. Then she saw the most incredible sight from the freeway: *Disneyland!* She was out of her mind with excitement but knew she couldn't blurt out anything like those "other" kids would do. She needed to be a proper little girl and just sit and wait. They pulled into the parking lot of the Disneyland Hotel, parked the car, and Aunt Betty said, "Ok, grab your suitcase. We're staying here. Aren't you excited?" "Yes, yes, Aunt Betty! Thank you!" The girl was out of her mind with happiness and joy. What a gift for this girl, like a fairy tale coming true. She hoped this would be the best trip with no slaps, no hangers, no pain of discipline.

Walking up to the check-in counter, Betty said they had a reservation under her name. Meadow was taking in everything she could: all the decorations, Disney characters she had seen on TV, hotel guests bustling around. It was overwhelming for a girl who was from a farm and a small town, to see so many sites. It was the most exciting thing Meadow had ever experienced—even better than Christmas!

The man behind the counter was handsome and seemed to be flirting with Betty. She gave him her best laugh when he cracked a little joke about some political thing. Meadow noticed this, but when the clerk said the amount that Aunt Betty owed for the room, Meadow blurted out, "Aunt Betty, we can't afford that!" Betty was frozen with embarrassment, only saying, "Oh honey, we can. It's ok." She pulled on the back of Meadow's hair hard enough to make the girl wince, doing it underneath her ponytail so no one noticed.

Betty paid and they grabbed their suitcases and walked to the elevator. They were alone going up to their floor, each of them quiet: one with quiet anger, the other with quiet fear. Meadow didn't dare ask to push the button to their floor. She heard most kids got to do that, but she knew the consequences of asking…worse yet, just going ahead and doing it without asking.

Getting to their room, Aunt Betty unlocked the door, opening it wide. The aroma of freshness was overwhelming. It was like one of those commercials on TV where they are trying to sell you the laundry detergent that has the best scent. Meadow knew what a true gift this was. She was a lucky girl.

There were twin beds, one for each of them. Betty put each suitcase on their own respective bed she had chosen for both. Then she told Meadow to take off her coat and turn around. Aunt Betty gave Meadow one of the most severe slaps she ever had, almost knocking her over. "Don't you ever embarrass me like that again! You have no idea about money, and you should know I would never take you on a trip if I couldn't afford it! I work hard to give you things that your parents never could." It was the same old story, putting down Meadow's parents so Betty would look like the savior, giving value to Meadow's life. Meadow's cheek was extremely red and hurt, but she was able to say "I'm sorry, Aunt Betty. I didn't mean to embarrass you." "Ok, honey, you know I love you and just want you to be raised right," Betty replied. Meadow said, "I know, Aunt Betty."

It was getting late, and with the Du-Par stop, neither of them was hungry. They changed into their night clothes, exchanged good nights with a kiss on the cheek, turned off the lights, and got into bed. Meadow hated to admit it, but Mary was right again. Her biggest hope for tomorrow at the magical place was that everyone and everything would run smoothly. The girl dreamed of dressed-up Disney characters parading around her, saying what a lovely, good girl she was over and over again.

They were up bright and early, got dressed, packed their things (as they were going to leave right after going to Disneyland), and headed down to the lobby for breakfast. Not a word was spoken about what happened the previous day. It was as if everything was normal, love flowing between the two. After breakfast, they loaded the car and headed for the monorail that would take them from the hotel to Disneyland itself.

For Meadow, this ride on the monorail was enough for her. Being high up and viewing the whole picture of Disneyland was beyond anything she had ever dreamed of. She was sure Mary would be jealous and couldn't wait to tell her all about the trip when she got home. They got their tickets and headed into the park, walking past the rows and rows of beautiful flowers. Although this setting was so much more, it reminded Meadow of Grama Janie's flower gardens on the ranch, a memory that would stay vivid in her mind at any age.

Getting into the park, Meadow noticed most of the kids were dressed in shorts, overalls, or pants, with just a shirt or blouse on. Most had comfy tennis shoes on as well. She was overdressed for sure. Her outfit was much "fancier," especially with her coat and black shoes. *My feet will be sore in no time*, she thought. But she knew her aunt always wanted her to look like a princess who was raised well, so nothing was mentioned. She knew the consequences of questioning her clothes.

Walking down Main Street, seeing all the shops, vendors, and all the nick knacks everywhere was an eyeful for the girl. It was almost too much to take in for little Meadow. Then she saw the cotton candy vendor. Before she could stop herself, she exclaimed, "Aunt Betty, look at the cotton candy!" The vendor was continually making the sugary treat, swirling the pink cloud into its final, luscious form. "Please can we have some?"

The moment the words came out of her mouth, she knew. Aunt Betty was holding Meadow's hand as usual, and stopped in her tracks, squeezing the girl's hand so tight it felt like the bones were going to crack. She got in front of Meadow, bent down to her level, and said quietly but with rage, "You know not to ask for anything. I've told you that repeatedly: good girls don't act like that, wanting everything they see." The woman had put her forehead right onto Meadow's forehead, pressing on it forcefully but not enough to knock her over. No one could really tell what was going on. It looked like Aunt Betty was trying to explain something to the girl.

"I'm sorry, Aunt Betty," Meadow said, as she always would. "I won't be a spoiled brat like other kids. I know you love me, and I'll be good." Betty said, "You better be, I worked hard for the money we've used on this trip." Truth was, Janie had given Betty a wad of her cash that she stored up from the various jobs she did. Without Janie's extra cash, the trip would not have happened.

The rest of the day was spent walking into the various lands, going on the Jungle Cruise, the Mad Hatter's Tea Party, Peter Pan's Flight, Snow White's Enchanted Wish, and a few others. Meadow loved it all and imagined herself being like some of the characters, flying, carefree and on her own doing what she wanted. She kept quiet and just followed Aunt Betty's lead.

They ate in one of the restaurants, and Meadow was allowed to buy one item at a store as they were walking out from the park. She chose a music box that had Snow White twirling in circles when you opened it. The beautiful music made the girl feel like a princess, as if she didn't have a care in the world. And for that minute, she didn't.

It got to be late afternoon, and it was time they got onto the freeway, making the trip home. Getting back on the monorail, they arrived back at the hotel. Once they got to the car, Meadow looked around, still in disbelief that this could happen to her. They traveled on the freeway, heading home. Neither of them spoke as they were both tired from the magical yet long day. Meadow was quiet mostly because she just didn't want any trouble. After a few hours of travel, the summer sun setting, they pulled in front of the house. Aunt Betty asked if Meadow had a good time. "Oh yes, Aunt Betty. Thank you so much for taking me. I know you worked hard for the money to take me," Meadow said. *Damn right, I did,* Betty thought. "You're welcome. You are a lucky girl. Not everyone has someone to take care of them and take them to such a beautiful place."

They went inside the house, and Pete and Janie were already fast asleep in their room. Meadow went in and kissed them on the cheek, Janie waking up and asking how it went. "You know, Grama, it was a fun time. I tried to be the best girl I could," Meadow said. Janie replied, "As long as you enjoyed yourself, that's what matters. Sleep tight."

Meadow went to her room, changed into her night clothes while Aunt Betty lay on the couch, and fell asleep dressed in what she had on. Meadow grabbed Mary, who asked, "Well, how'd it go? Was I right?" "We'll talk about it tomorrow. I'm too tired to explain," Meadow said as she kissed the doll, turned out the light, and fell fast asleep.

The Disney characters came back into Meadow's dream, repeating that she was a smart and good girl, who deserved the trip and shouldn't let all the other things she was disciplined for bother her. The characters said to her, "That aunt can't do that forever to you... You'll be safe someday and loved."

As time went on, the constant "overseeing" by Aunt Betty was something Meadow learned to accept for her basic survival. She did her homework, completed any chores or things that were asked of her, and enjoyed all her classmates and nuns at school. Meadow learned how to play the game to handle this woman. In this respect, Meadow had wisdom about how different personalities worked at a young age, which was a benefit throughout her whole life. Most people take others at face value: what you see is what you get. But Meadow could "size someone up" right away and play their game that would gather favor with them.

Grama Janie continually guided Meadow to "fib" now and then to Aunt Betty, telling her a small lie here and there. Janie would say, "Don't let your aunt know that," or, "Let's keep that between us two," winking at Meadow with a look of protection. This was necessary for everyone's survival, not just Meadow's. It kept that boat from rocking…better yet, from turning over.

This formed an alliance of protection with Janie that taught Meadow lessons in life about people. While Janie didn't realize that this was what she was doing, it gave Meadow a strong base to survive crises that eventually enter everyone's lives. Either you fight, get organized, and handle things, or you wither away and lose your foothold.

27

HIGH SCHOOL FOLLIES

BEING IN A CATHOLIC SCHOOL environment was all Meadow ever knew. While the nuns and rules were strict, in certain ways the experience was the same cocoon of protection that she got from Grama Janie and Grampa Pete. She learned to follow orders, be good, go to mass, and receive the sacraments. Friends were endeared who lasted a lifetime, friends she could rely on and have fun with. Meadow became the social one among her friends with lots laughing and being a bit goofy at times. They all loved this and couldn't wait for recess to see what was going to happen. Meadow always fulfilled her duty of being "the fun one."

The fortunate thing was that Meadow was developing a personality you wouldn't think could happen with Aunt Betty's disciplinary style. But Meadow's experiences ended up making her stronger, developing a personality that gravitated people to her. This became something Betty despised in Meadow because she was—for the most part—jealous. Although Betty had beauty and a way of interacting with people, Betty was still a wallflower at heart. She had no use for any woman who was outgoing or boisterous. But if a man acted in that manner, she thought they had a "good personality" and was a "go ahead, strong" kind of man.

Meadow went through grade school, ultimately getting good enough grades for Betty, enjoying her friends and extended family. Aunt Betty's physical abuse began to slow down as Meadow was now about her size as well. The woman became aware that she needed to guide the girl with more verbal "suggestions," using a somewhat pleasantly authoritative tone. Her niece was wise to this and let Aunt Betty talk without really listening, responding, "Oh yes, Aunt Betty, I agree." Meadow came to terms with Aunt Betty's ways and did the best to ignore her. The constant verbal correcting, like, "Sit up straight. Slouching makes you look like your weak and not paying attention," or "Have you put on a little weight? Those pants seem tight," and "That hairstyle doesn't look good on you. Your hair is way too thin and straight to pull it off like those other girls" was a constant reminder for Meadow to not think too highly of herself. Degrading Meadow in different ways was the lady's latest way of continually having control of something in her life. Betty did this as if it was so natural, engrained in her being. Without knowing about Patrick and Leroy in her aunt's and mother's lives, Meadow was positive something terrible happened to them in their childhood.

Meadow graduated grade school and went on to the Catholic high school in the area. This was what Aunt Betty wanted so Pete and Janie went along with the idea even though tuition was involved. Meadow's education was important to them, so there was no question about spending the money. Many of Meadow's fellow students were attending the same school, so she felt the comradery would be good.

Going through her freshman year at this school, Meadow and her best friend, Sarah, decided they were tired of the Catholic prayers and customs attached to a parochial school. They begged their families to change to public high school for their next three years. Their families agreed, mostly because there was no tuition attached to public school. The two friends were ecstatic and ready for a new adventure, an opportunity that would change their lives forever. While Betty was hesitant, she also gave the ok. She and Virginia had gone to that school, and *We turned out ok,* she thought. *Well, at least I did…*

Meadow started public high school and loved it. Compared to the Catholic high school, there were so many different types of kids—some athletes, some nerds, and a lot of types in between. Drugs were beginning to be the norm is some groups, especially marijuana. It was the late 1960s so there were groups that were more of the "hippie" type. These kids were spinoffs from the beatnik era that recently was fading out of style.

Right away, Meadow made new friends, developing an updated version of herself. Having friends in each group and relating to them all, Meadow gained popularity across the board.

Most of the kids her age from the neighborhood went to the public high school, so there was a core friendship already on campus. She felt free, able to entice an audience with her funny voices and jokes. It had been the right decision to get away from the Catholic agenda she had experienced for so many school years, exposing her to a world that was around her, yet had gone unnoticed by Meadow because of Aunt Betty's constraints.

Every morning, Uncle Raymond would stop by their house in his truck to pick up Pete to work on the ranch where they raised their steers. Raymond would have a cup of coffee, shoot the breeze with Pete and Janie, and relax a bit before their workday began. He would arrive before Meadow left for school so he could enjoy her before she left. When they moved to town from the ranch, he stayed with Pete and Janie for a bit. Then he bought himself a house a few miles away, eventually getting married but never had any children. His wife, Aleksandra, was from Poland with a heavy accent and forceful personality. She had been held at an encampment in Auschwitz with numbers tattooed on the inside of her arm. She didn't share how she escaped or the true story behind it all but had come out of the experience as a fighter rather than dwelling on her previous life. Raymond was a direct, in charge man on the ranch, but when it came to Aleksandra, he was puddy in her hands.

It was unclear where they met. Rumer had it that she put a gun to his head and forced him to marry her after a brief romance. No one asked, they just accepted Aleksandra, and that was that. With no children of his own, Raymond stayed very close to Meadow, always wanting to protect her. The family never shared with him the discipline the girl received from Betty. They knew his temper would get the best of him and who knows what the consequences would be. He always figured that after the episode with little Meadow washing the dishes at the ranch, Betty behaved much better with the girl.

Betty had finally moved to the family's town, renting an apartment not far away from Meadow and the grandparents. Every day before Betty went to her bookkeeping job she had gotten in town, she'd stop by the house before the girl went to school, checking things out, and surveying the situation, still trying to rule and guide her niece. Those days were numbered for sure, a sign of positive independence that Meadow was gaining year by year.

Betty walked into the house saying, "Good morning, everyone." The lady was decked out as usual, looking beautiful with her dark hair, new styled clothes, and pumps. She had meticulously applied makeup that matched what she was wearing. She had noticed Uncle Raymond's truck in front of the house, so she knew everyone was on time. Betty headed to the small kitchen with the same appliances and setup as when George and Virginia called this house their home. Pete and Raymond were drinking coffee at the yellow Formica kitchen table, joking about political things or people they knew.

Ever the worker, Janie was at the sink washing dishes. The electric coffee pot sat on a small counter to the left in the kitchen, with cabinets above. The small dining room that Raymond had used as a bedroom and where Baby Jean had enjoyed that soft, summer breeze was through an opening in the kitchen just past the coffee counter.

Meadow had come out from her bedroom, dressed, ready for school, and leaning against the refrigerator. As Betty was grabbing her coffee from the counter where the coffee was percolating, she looked over at Meadow standing in the doorway of the dining room. Betty's eyes got wide, and she yelled, "Take off that Goddamn dress! You look like a cheap slut!"

Calmly stepping up to her, Meadow grabbed the aunt, shoved her against the refrigerator in a choke hold, yelling, "I'm fifteen and I'll dress any way I want!" The shock in the aunt's eyes was new to the girl. Never had she physically gone against the lady, and that *taste* of freedom was incredible. After all, the dress was totally in style: soft, sheer voile fabric, small flower pattern, a peplum skirt, and puffed short sleeves. With platform shoes and nylons, she wore that outfit like it was meant to be worn. True, the dress barely covered the girl's butt, but Meadow thought, *When you look good, you look good. Time to set this bitch straight!*

As Meadow abruptly let go of Betty, she nonchalantly turned around, looking over to her grandparents and Raymond and said, "Bye, see you after school. I'm going out to wait for my ride." Sarah was Meadow's ride to and from school, having bought a Volkswagen Bug a few months before. Meadow grabbed her books and purse and headed out. Sarah pulled up a few minutes later. Getting into the car, Meadow looked over at Sarah and yelled, "I just took care of that fucking bitch! Yah!" Sarah laughed out loud, and off they went.

Sarah was one of the few friends of Meadow's who understood Aunt Betty's abuse, not judging her friend for feeling the way she did. She came from a household with a drunken, crazed father and a submissive mother. Her father was white, of German descent while her mother was Filipino. He had that macho idea he was superior to his wife, demanding she be subservient to him. When she wasn't, all drunken hell would break loose, with hitting and screaming between the two. Sarah retreated to Meadow when this abuse would go on. The two girls were confidants that relied on each other for moral support. When Meadow complained to other friends about Betty's behavior, they told her she was "spoiled" and lucky to have her in her life. Understanding this, she trusted only Sarah with her Aunt Betty experiences.

Betty started to go after her, but then Raymond stepped in and stopped her, saying, "Leave the girl alone!" Betty stopped in her tracks, went back to the counter to grab her purse, and left for work. No more was said. The three left in the house were glad this happened, not realizing it was finally the start of Meadow's life of independence. Yet this small victory could never erase the years of stern talking to, slaps, hanger beatings, rule after rule, penalties if not followed. Those feelings might never go away. But this was a beginning to the freedom that Meadow so deserved and yearned for, giving her more strength to combat Aunt Betty's verbal *guidance* that would never go away.

28

WINGS OF FREEDOM

TEENAGE YEARS CAN BE THE best or worst time in someone's life. Puberty happens, with emotions and socialization becoming more and more evident. For Meadow, it was a wonderful part of her life, and she grabbed on to this time with a zest like no other, fully grasping these limited few years in her life. She was experiencing some freedom from Aunt Betty's hold, and she vowed that nothing would get in the way of her happiness. Her childhood memories of Aunt Betty's discipline were still there, tucked in a place where she would not let them be the focus of her life. But the mental abuse continued for years, the constant beratement proving to be worse than the physical pain she inflicted during Meadow's childhood.

While Meadow had a couple of boyfriends early on, her true love, Jamey, was an unexpected find. She was a sophomore, and he was a senior. They had mutual friends that set them up to go out and spend some time getting to know each other. While Meadow had continued her gregarious personality, Jamey was quieter and more reflective. The year was 1969, and the "peace-and-love" hippie movement was gaining momentum, replacing the beatnik generation of the 1950s and early 1960s. The Vietnam War had been going on for some years, a seemingly senseless war that took tens of thousands of US lives, with many of the wounded soldiers suffering long-term mental and physical health issues. The Army's use of Agent Orange to remove vegetation from the dense Vietnam jungles revealed itself to be a fatal toxin some years later as well. This war caused unrest across the country and the world with hundreds of protests in many major cities, especially in San Francisco. The city became a hub for the hippie way of life, with the Haight-Ashbury area of the city being a super charged location for all of this. A change was coming with a resistance to the status quo that challenged conservative America.

Jamey resonated with this philosophy of peace, writing romantic poems to Meadow expressing his feelings of love. The young man wanted to have longer hair, emulating the style that was becoming popular in the world. Since he always worked, he couldn't let his hair grow any longer than just over his ears. Even as short as his hair was, some of Meadow's family thought Jamey was a definite hippie because his hair wasn't trimmed short. Humorous when one thinks about it, especially with today's hair styles being all over the map. But they were a conservative family group who only wanted the best for Meadow.

Jamey also came from a Swiss Italian farming dairy family, so Pete and Janie were ecstatic that the couple started seeing each other. Jamey would come over for dinner and then on Sunday for breakfast. Meadow and Jamey spent every moment they could together, driving in the surrounding country, listening to Kenny Loggins and Jim Messina; Crosby, Stills, Nash & Young; James Taylor; and other great music from that time. With Jamey writing Meadow beautiful poems she cherished, Jamey was unlike any other boy she knew. He opened her eyes to more of the world than she would have been aware of otherwise.

This romance was not the choice Aunt Betty would have picked for Meadow. The aunt wanted Meadow to go out with a burly football player, a manly man, macho, in control. It was the type of man Betty wanted for herself, thinking that's how it should be. "You can't have this soft-spoken hippie as your boyfriend! I don't care what kind of family he comes from; I want you to be with a *real* man," Betty would insist. "Someone who is tall and handsome, someone to whisk you off your feet, that wears a football letterman's jacket, polite yet manly!" They had repeated arguments over this relationship, very heated, almost to the point of physical harm. Betty just couldn't help herself from trying to control one more thing in the girl's life, creating a larger crevice between them, turning a beginning crack into a full valley. The girl's independence was at stake, and Meadow was not going to let the aunt ruin her happiness.

29

LOVE WINS

AFTER DATING FOR A COUPLE years, Jamey asked Meadow to marry him. At twenty and nineteen, they were young, even by the standards of the 1970s. Most people had begun waiting till after college to get married, getting their career going before making this lifelong decision. Jamey finished two years of community college and had taken his dream job at a plant-growing nursery an hour south. Meadow went to community college for one year, then decided she'd rather work to make her own money, helping at a popular gift shop downtown. Their future together was going to begin. Living together would have been frowned upon by their families, and never really discussed between Jamey and Meadow. It was marriage or nothing.

Once Aunt Betty got wind of the marriage, she was in high gear to get it stopped. *Marry this guy?* she thought. *No way! I will not allow that to happen and let the girl ruin her life!* Betty confronted Meadow with all the force she had in the living room of the grandparents' house. The beige couch was long, against the west wall, with pillows on each end, the perfect place to have this argument. Aunt Betty tried to talk Meadow out of the marriage, saying all kinds of rude things about Jamey. Betty yelled, "He's not forceful; he's way too gentle to take care of you. And he will take you away from us to another city, where he's just going to work at a nursery and not be a businessman like you need. No way, I won't let that happen!"

The girl's rage got the best of her, and they finally got in a physical push and pull confrontation. Meadow scratched Betty's face, pushed her onto the couch, and yelled, "I will marry who I want, and you can't tell me I can't. Grama, Grampa, and Mom (Meadow knew including Virginia in this would make Betty even angrier) love Jamey, they are happy for me and said I can have any wedding I want. And since you don't like my choice, I won't let you have any part of the planning of this day for us… I will do it all myself!" Meadow loved Jamey and wanted to marry him, and there was this huge part of her that just couldn't avoid *turning the knife* when it came to hurting Aunt Betty. It was one more act of defiant freedom the girl needed to continue her mode of survival from the aunt's clutches, making her stronger with each challenge.

Janie and Pete were just happy that Meadow was marrying somebody they liked and respected, someone from their own "neck of the woods," you might say. He was not a bragging, think-I'm-better-than-you type of person to love their granddaughter. That meant more to them than all the money in the world. So, the wedding plans began. Meadow was in high gear to make sure this was the most beautiful wedding she could create. Since neither of their daughters had weddings, Pete and Janie beamed with pride that they could invite friends and relatives to celebrate this special event.

Meadow did everything herself, organizing every detail. For a teenager at that time, this was quite a feat. She would turn nineteen by the time the wedding took place, but her maturity about things was way beyond her years. After being with Jamey, Meadow had grown more into her personality, learning much more about herself. She now had an ally who would protect her against Betty, while not judging Virginia or the rest of the family. That was huge for Meadow, and she loved him more for this.

Pete and Janie were happy to pay for everything, writing checks for the necessary wedding things: flowers, venue, food, etc. While she hadn't expressed this fact, Meadow had an eye for style, along with the small details that go along with that eye. Pete's family had saved Edie Grama's wedding dress with the hopes someone in the family would wear it for their special day. Since she had loved Grama Edie (she had passed some years ago), Meadow was thrilled at the prospect of this, but the dress had gotten weathered and stained in storage. Being an industrious girl, Meadow found a seamstress who could copy the dress, changing a few things for practicality. The look of the dress was vintage late 1800s, with a top and skirt embellished with lace, satin, and pearls, and dictated the style of the rest of the wedding. The attendants wore velvet dusty rose-colored dresses, with bib styled lace tops and sleeves with period riding hats to complete the look. Rather than traditional bouquets to carry, Meadow nailed the finished look deciding the girls should carry closed umbrellas, the flowers cascading out from them. The men were dressed in tuxedos, pin striped vests, and ascot type ties. Held in a small, Catholic country church, the wedding went off beautifully, with lots of food, dancing, and fun times. Betty was invited to the wedding, but she did not have a say in any decisions. In fact, Meadow decided not to speak to Betty until the actual day of the wedding. Meadow's independence was on the rise.

This little girl was now a blossoming adult, and while Aunt Betty frowned at the "spectacle wedding," no one cared what she thought. She felt it was a braggy occasion, trying to show off as if the family had money. *We're just working people,* she thought. *Not rich like some of these farming folks.* She brought this up many times to Janie leading up to the event. Janie told her not to worry about it; they were paying for it and loved helping their sweet Meadow. Of course, Betty was dressed beautifully for the occasion, spreading her warm smile and gracious ways, acting as if she was partially responsible for the beautifully executed wedding. Aunt Betty's constant discipline, keeping Meadow "in line," did ultimately contribute to the young woman's ability to put the wedding pieces together. Meadow had been determined to pull this off without Betty's help and the final event proved she could. Pete and Janie were proud to walk down that aisle, viewing all their friends and relatives sharing in their blessings. Virginia beamed as well, seeing that light being focused on her baby Meadow. She was her mother no matter what and loved basking in the attention spotlight.

Now Meadow was able to escape and move away to start her own life, with the bad memories staying at bay for a while. Yet she would still hear the whisper of Aunt Betty's voice in her ear, *you aren't as smart as them, your hair is too thin, have you put on weight?, he won't be able to take care of you, your parents didn't love you and gave you up, we're all you have.* These words were a haunting reminder that Aunt Betty's discipline might never, never go away.

30

NEW LIFE ADULTS

THE YOUNG COUPLE MOVED TO their cottage in the small beach town and hour south. They lived life, met new people who had no idea of their background, who enjoyed them for who they were, not where they came from. It was a life neither of them had ever experienced. They embraced this period with memories that they cherished for life.

Meadow and Jamey enjoyed this beach town for a few years, but they ended up getting homesick and wanted to buy a house. Meadow was naive to think being miles away from her aunt would keep the woman at a distance: her presence would be around no matter what. So, the couple moved back to their hometown, bought a house, and both went to work. The house was perfect for them with a detached garage, natural wood wainscotting, a stone fireplace, two bedrooms, and two bathrooms. It was like the universe was watching over them. Aunt Betty was still in their lives, charming her way with everyone else, but still being judgmental with Meadow.

Aunt Betty never said things to Meadow in front of Jamey, so he didn't fully understand the damage this woman had done to his wife. A bit later, he finally understood the impact that Betty had on Meadow, so he made every attempt to shield Meadow and their family. There would be no more physical abuse for sure; but the deep-rooted damage from early years was ever present in Meadow's brain, holding onto her disgust for Aunt Betty. These feelings did help to shield her from further, deep-seated damage.

Jamey and Meadow had two beautiful children: a boy, Theo, and a girl, Melissa. When Theo was born, the attending nurse gushed over the boy calling him "Little Robert Redford" as he had the perfect shaped face, almost as if he hadn't gone through any birth trauma. When Melissa was born, the same nurse fell in love with her. "What a perfect little girl, petite with perfectly formed features. And what a sweet smile!" The children were born two-and-a-half years apart, perfect timing to raise together in the household. Diaper changing would overlap for these close years, but then all of that would be over.

When Melissa was born, Meadow's past started to resurface in her mind. Her early years of being severely disciplined weren't usually present in her daily life, but now she couldn't stop thinking about the abuse she endured and went into severe postpartum depression. In so many cases, abuse continues with each generation, and this became a huge fear for Meadow. With no outside guidance, Meadow innately knew how to be a quality mother, caring for Theo in a positive way. But now she was depressed for days at a time. While she was able to care for both children, she couldn't stop worrying she would start abusing her children and not be able to take care of them properly. This thought did come up every now and then after she got married, but she immediately dismissed this as overthinking, letting her common sense take over.

Meadow's mind would start racing, thinking, *Will I hurt my children like I was hurt? Can I be patient and not get angry over situations that come up? If this does happen, how do I stop it?* Jamey was a bit oblivious to all this, not having a clue about what was happening. He made time to come home for lunch to see how everyone was. The children were asleep, with Meadow sitting on the floor in the living area surrounded by toys and other baby things. "Jamey, I need help!" Meadow said in a panic. "Should I call your mother to come over to help?" he responded. Virginia had babysat on occasion, and, for some reason, Meadow trusted Virginia, even though her psychosis would reveal itself at times. An emphatic "No!" was Meadow's answer. Virginia would probably whine, "Now you know how it feels!" taking a long drag from her cigarette, its toxic smoke floating into the air.

Jamey knew better than to suggest Aunt Betty. Betty probably would have said, "Oh, Meadow, please don't turn out like your mother! Just force yourself to get things done. Don't be lazy!" And Grama Janie was busy cleaning houses for other people to bring in extra money, showing her value in the world. Mentioning this to any of them was out of the question, along with any of Jamey's family. Meadow felt all alone on this island of despair.

They decided to call a good friend to help Meadow during the day, someone nonjudgmental, understanding what was going on. Jamey helped at night with feedings, changing diapers, and walking around holding each child to keep them calm, rocking them to go back to sleep.

Slowly things got better, and Meadow knew in her heart she would never harm her children, only having the most love for them. Jamey could breathe easier knowing things were being taken care of in the right way. Although he did his best, he didn't have the tools to know how to help with this, nor could he completely understand what was going on in Meadow's mind. His life had been different, and this was so foreign to him. In Meadow's family, they kept confidential family matters private, so finally asking for help meant she really needed that help. Fortunately, Meadow let that all go and began to feel much happier, getting on with her life. The children were safe, and the family could move on.

They lived and worked, making sure these children were shielded from Betty in a way that no harm would come to them. Betty was allowed to be in their life, but they never let her babysit or care for them. Betty rationalized this by thinking, *My working job is important, so there is no time for taking care of those kids!*

While Jamey wasn't totally aware of the level of abuse that Meadow had endured over the years, he understood that *something* had happened in her childhood for Meadow to have such hatred for Aunt Betty. It wasn't brought up very much, but there were times when something would flash a memory to the surface. Meadow would catch her hair on something and say, "Ouch! That reminds me of when Aunt Betty would pull my hair in stores if I looked at things too much." Or Meadow would accidentally bump her head on something, causing pain and leaving a bruise. Jamey would question what happened, and Meadow would say, "I hit my head on the corner of the cabinet. You know, just like when Aunt Betty would grab my blouse collar, shake me, and bounce me off a kitchen cabinet. Boy did that hurt! Sometimes I couldn't keep my little mouth shut. She'd give me a slap as well just to make sure I kept in line."

Meadow would mention these situations so nonchalantly, as if it was just something that happened in everyday life for most people. Little by little, the picture of Betty's abuse of Meadow became clearer to Jamey. He never confronted Betty about these things happening, realizing that her "sweet" demeanor to his face would deny any physical harm, saying, "Oh, that Meadow makes up stories. I would never hurt her… You know that, Jamey." He knew the physical abuse was in the past. It needed to stay there until Meadow brought it up and wanted to talk about it. His job was to be there, supporting Meadow with love and understanding.

31

DEFIANT FINALE

VIRGINIA LIVED IN THE AREA for the rest of her life. She would rent apartments, get county help, and receive money from her parents. Her living situations usually came with a problem Virginia manifested: a loud neighbor, rats coming in, cold air leaking from windows, on and on. She had the ability of befriending people for her own gain, getting them on her side, defending her no matter what. She basically did this to spite her family, stating "I have friends, so fuck you all." Even with Meadow and her family she became increasingly distant, not showing up for certain holidays, events. Always invited, she'd pick and choose what she attended, her not showing up was another way of announcing "I can do what I want, when I want." Virginia's behavior was understood by Meadow and the family as just how it was with Virginia. *Let her be, she'll come when she wants to.*

Virginia's defiant independence became a constant theme in her life. Baby Jean's death, Meadow being "taken away" from her and George, rationalizing this fact as it was all her family's fault, not blaming herself, adding to her psychosis and hallucinations. After years of smoking, Virginia developed severe emphysema. She kept begging her doctor to prescribe a mobile oxygen tank that she could attach to her nostrils, breathing better from her shortness of breath that became a constant problem. She would go into the doctor's office, breathing heavily, dramatically coughing as if she was ready to die at any time. The nurses would roll their eyes at each other, seeing this scenario with every visit. Although the doctor knew much of this was an act, he decided an oxygen tank was the right thing to prescribe. "Thank you, doctor," Virginia whispered with her cute smile and that twinkle in her eyes. "I really need this, and you've helped me so much." He replied, "You are welcomed, Virginia. Now, realize you need to quit smoking, and if you don't, this is a waste of time for all of us. I want you to feel good and enjoy life." "Of course, doctor," she sweetly replied. "I appreciate this so much."

Once she got into her car to go pick up the oxygen tank, she lit up a cigarette. "You are not going to tell me how to live, doc. I need this oxygen, and I can smoke as well!" Such defiance became her only way of survival. She used the system, didn't care who got in the way, and was going to live her own life. Virginia would walk around her upstairs apartment, going out to the balcony to smoke her Camel non-filters, the trusty oxygen tank at her side with air flowing into her nostrils. She didn't care one bit that an oxygen tank and smoking do not go hand in hand. Virginia would toss her head back as always, slowly and fiercely inhaling the smoke, letting that smoke flow into the breezy fresh air. *She* was in charge, and that was that.

Virginia's life clock was ticking, her mental illness severely taking over after years of battling the demons that engulfed her life. Obstinate to the end, she called 9-1-1 repeatedly to take her to the hospital because she couldn't breathe. The county finally had to step in and do a 5150, declaring her mentally unfit to be around herself and others. The family could not (nor wanted to) step in to stop this. Virginia was taken to a facility in Southern California where patients were cared for as best as they could be under current law and circumstances, much less cruel than the hospital she was taken to fifty years previously. Meadow was able to connect with the facility to find out about coming to see her mother. They did allow certain visiting hours, and Virginia agreed to see her daughter.

Meadow and a friend drove the three hours to the hospital, only to be told that her mother now refused to see her. This wasn't unexpected, as Meadow knew her mother's obstinate behavior. She forgave her and let it go. Virginia became severely bulimic, refusing other visitors, being in control for one last time. She laid in her bed, withering away at a mere sixty pounds, dreaming of the good times with George, the birth of Meadow, and a life filled with love and happiness that had no judgment or ridicule, no fiery devil face of Leroy. She passed peacefully at the age of sixty-eight.

The family had not fought this, realizing how angry and resistant Virginia would be. Meadow helped her when possible, having sadness about the tragic things that had happened to her mother. Virginia was a part of her grandchildren's lives, and they called her "Grama Virgie," understanding she had quirky ways but still loving her for those ways. Virginia was now at peace, the psychosis drifting away into space. The family could finally breathe easy. Being the *loving* sister, Betty organized a beautiful funeral for Virginia, showing the extended family what good, caring people they were. Pete and Janie gladly paid for this. They bought a crypt at the same mausoleum close to where Baby Jean was resting. They could finally live their lives knowing their girl Virginia was in a better place. No struggling to be heard, no fighting life, no bickering between sisters—just a quiet life for everyone.

32

BETTY AND EARL

WITH MEADOW'S LIFE TRAVELING ON, and Virginia finally out of her life, Betty focused on work and her social life. Along with being involved with her extended family (aunts, uncles, cousins), getting out and interacting with the world seemed to be her salvation. Her relationships with men did last for a few years here and there but the bonds wouldn't stand the test of time. Whether it was due to her lack of physically romantic interaction or something else hidden that only these men saw, it's difficult to know.

Betty had a close friend, Lucielle, she met at a company picnic. She was a relative of one of Betty's coworkers and the ladies hit it off immediately. She was a boisterous, fun lady, unlike Betty who had been *quietly* fun most of her life. This friendship was an asset to Betty's life. Lucielle was always wanting to do things, dragging Betty here and there for fun, and single as well. The woman was always on "the prowl" to find them both a good man they could grab onto and take for a ride.

The duo would frequent local bars after their workday, having a few drinks, laughing and interacting with any men that were there. Lucielle had long, dark wavy hair that she tousled back and forth, especially when men were around, interacting with light, funny conversation. There were many farmers and cowboys in the area and Lucille gravitated toward that western style of dressing, usually wearing large, dangling earrings. She would laugh loudly and was a social magnate wherever she went. Normally, this type of forceful woman would be shunned by Betty and complained about. But in Lucielle's case, she enjoyed every minute with her.

One evening they were at a small, local bar. It was one of those dark places where people could forget themselves drinking the night away doing whatever they wanted and not being noticed. It was a weeknight, so the ladies hadn't planned on staying out late. This one man kept looking at Betty and she would smile back. He finally went over and sat by her, buying her and Lucielle a cocktail. Betty was her happy, fun self that most people saw, still physically beautiful and styled perfectly for the times. They chatted, flirted, and the man was enchanted by this lovely, fun woman. His name was Earl and he was from Missouri, miles away from his original stomping grounds. He had been in the Air Force, then landed at the Air Force Base close by, being on the on-site firemen team. Earl was divorced with one teenage son that lived with his family in Missouri. The man was free to live the way he wanted, nothing to tie him down and was searching for a nice woman to enjoy life and have fun with. Betty did seem to fit the bill: beautiful, laughed at his jokes, had a good job and her own money. Earl started falling for her and their relationship seemed to be on an upward swing.

For years Betty had put down Virginia's George for having one of those Oklahoma accents, saying, "How backward it sounds, not having one bit of class when he speaks," and "Why would Virginia marry such an Okey?! So like her to pick someone who talks like that." Lo and behold, Earl had that same type of twang accent from Missouri. Meadow saw a chance to come back at Betty, reminding her what she had said about her faither. In her most defensive response, she said: "I never would say that! I love how Earl talks." Meadow just shook her head, knowing exactly how Aunt Betty would defend her new friend.

Earl and Betty dated for about a year. For some reason she didn't reveal much to the family about this relationship. She was going out, seeing someone, but not serious. With her romantic history not being the success she would want, it was probably smart not to expect this to go anywhere. But that darn clock was ticking away. Her niece was married and didn't seem to need her, Pete and Janie were in good shape living their lives, and Virginia was gone to not be embarrassed about.

Earl wasn't her ideal man. Her dream was to have a Paul Newman type: tall, handsome, sweep-you-off-your feet guy to spend her life with. One of her loves had been that type and Betty was devastated when he hit the road. Coming out of that relationship took her a few years. It was time to make the dive and get on with her life. Betty and Earl decided to get married, and a Lake Tahoe, Nevada wedding was quick and done. Their life together had started. They lived in his paid-for house with mostly his furniture and some of her things. What seemed to be an idyllic life for them became something neither of them planned.

33

RELATIVE TIMING

YEARS TRAVELED ON AS THEY do, with everyone passing away except for Betty, Earl and Raymond. With Pete, Janie and Viginia all gone along with most of the great-aunts and -uncles, the two were always included in Meadow's family gatherings and holidays, along with Jamey's mother, Darlene and stepfather, Frederick. Meadow and her family were the only immediate family members left. While Betty was in Theo and Melissa's lives, Meadow would never allow her to take care of them or be left alone with her. This fact was never mentioned, just understood that this was the way things were. With Aunt Betty's *discipline style*, Meadow made sure Theo and Melissa were protected from her slaps and hanger beatings. Betty would watch her Ps and Qs around the children and these gatherings, always saying the right thing in a sweet voice, chatting about politics, the weather, current styles. Then she would corner Meadow in the kitchen, saying derogatory things about whoever else was there, usually in the Swiss dialect her parents used.

"She's so stupid," Betty would say about Jamey's mom. "And Jamey's stepfather, such a prick!" That sweet demeanor would go away when talking to her niece alone. "Oh, Meadow, you should know better than that. You were taught well," or "You really have put on some weight, haven't you?" whispered in her ear. Aunt Betty continued trying to have mental control over Meadow. It was naturally engrained in her being to be this way, still thinking of her niece as *that little girl* she needed to be molded into someone who wasn't going to be like those parents of hers, George and

Virginia. Every chance she could, Betty would try some belittling remark in the hope of having that same control she had over young Meadow.

Meadow would almost have a panic attack before each situation involving Aunt Betty. Seeking professional help, Meadow had a safe place to relay her memories and fears. The counselor would repeatedly suggest the same theme, "You need to keep her out of your life as much as possible." The idea seemed simple, solving that lifelong pain. Uprooting Meadow's family and moving to another location would not solve the problem. Because Meadow was taught respect and helping when needed, she could not give herself permission to abandon this lady. Aunt Betty was in her life till the end.

Earl ended up despising Betty who revealed her true self to him more over the years. He could see her ignorance about money, always trying to look a certain way in public when the reality was that she was as fake as they came. It was later discovered he had physically abused Betty, a bruise here, a fall there. He became more of a drinker, with history repeating itself like Virginia's life. Betty would never, never, admit any of this, painting a picture-perfect relationship for her and Earl. What saved their relationship was that she cared for different relatives over the years. She would work, and then she would go take care of the relative living at their home. The appearance was that Betty was the giver and had to do this. After all, who else was there? The last was Uncle Raymond who she lived with and cared for after his wife, Aleksandra, died. She lived with him for some years until he passed away as well, which was the end of the line of the aunts and uncles to care for.

34

THE DAISY TRAIN

BETTY CONTINUED TO CARE FOR Raymond until he passed. As he never had children of his own, he left Betty the house and its rental in the back area of yard, all his belongings and any money. She continued living in the house and left everything as it was: his clothes remained where they were, along with food, furnishings, even his toothbrush stayed in the cup on the bathroom counter. She stayed living there thinking of the house as a monument to Raymond that needed to be guarded, watched over.

Earl was happy to live apart from Betty. Having retired a few years earlier, he had a great pension and had no money problems whatsoever. He didn't have to think about divorce, going through the expense and trouble, dividing furniture and things. "Let her rot over there," Earl would say in his Missouri twang, "I'll be just fine." This kept things civil and very separate, each living the way they wanted. Holidays would be spent at Meadow's house, both coming together with their dessert to add to the meal. Nothing was said about separate living. It was understood that's how it was.

Down the block from Raymond's house was a family with the cutest little girl, Daisy, who Betty got very close to. She'd walk down daily to say hello and spend some time having conversations about anything they'd like, sharing in their life. Betty had retired, with lots of time on her hands, never developing any hobbies or forms of recreation. "My life is too busy always working and taking care of family," she'd say. "I don't have time for any of that nonsense."

The Betty that Daisy and her family knew was this giving, happy, cordial human being. She became extremely close to Daisy, and the girl began calling her "grandma." Daisy and her family became like Betty's second family, never revealing much about her *real* family to them. The young girl filled a void Betty had in her life. Her relationship with Earl was not what she had hoped, and Meadow kept her at arm's length, her memories not completely letting go of their past. Her niece was there if she needed anything, but it wasn't the relationship she wanted: closeness to another human being.

As years went by, Betty's relationship with Daisy grew closer. Daisy was getting ready for college and Betty told the girl and her family she wanted to help with her college tuition and living expenses, ending up paying for it all. Betty decided to take out a loan on the paid-for house she inherited from her uncle to help Daisy with college expenses and whatever else she needed. This was a young girl who only knew one side of this person, who gave her as much attention as Betty wanted with no history, no questions. It was that unconditional love Betty craved so badly, which she couldn't get from her immediate family because of the past. They knew her true being and she couldn't hide it from them any longer. Since the house was paid for, it was a large sum of money that she could borrow. She had great credit, her income was solid, which made the loan easy to procure. Meadow knew nothing about this loan, nor should she necessarily. Like most people, Betty had always been very secretive about any of her money, investments, or retirement. She gave the impression she was in good financial shape as she could retire and live.

This loan was the start of her economic drain, a spiral that could not be stopped, which created a domino effect of financial ruin. The payment was a considerable amount with higher interest attached and was taken out when home loans were given to anybody just before the real estate crash of 2008. Along with that, Betty's entire retirement portfolio was lost by a local investor she trusted with all her money who invested in high-risk real estate like so many did. In one instant, she had nothing in retirement, no money coming in but her social security. Betty couldn't keep up with the loan payment, but she was still living there and only getting payment from the rental when the tenant felt like paying, which would go on for months at a time.

With social security her only money to live on, Betty survived as best she could. The house inevitably went into foreclosure with Betty not fully understanding the consequences of not paying your mortgage. After all, it was her house, Uncle Raymond left it to her. How could they take it away? A real estate friend of Meadow's saw the foreclosure in the local newspaper. She called Meadow, and they jumped into action. There was still time to stop the foreclosure if they could sell the property and pay back the loan or work out something with the loan company. Betty had ignored the notices she received, even the letters that were sent certified mail that she had signed for. It was as if this was all a dream, Betty not grasping the true reality of the situation. Meadow and the friend went to the house to talk to Aunt Betty. She reluctantly let them in. The realtor explained everything, with Betty's reply being, "This won't happen. I'm not selling this house!"

Betty had a perfect credit rating, and a foreclosure would plumet that rating. Her stubborn determination led her to believe she could get out of this. Everything else had been financially taken care of in her life, so why not this? Betty refused to sell the property and eventually got locked out of the house by the sheriffs. They did let her go inside to take her personal belongings, but that was it. This whole situation didn't make sense to Meadow. It was as if Aunt Betty had a disconnect in her brain about the reality of what was happening. There were no signs of dementia—just an awareness of someone whose fear couldn't live in the reality of what was happening.

She never let Meadow know what she did with the money, why a loan was taken out on that paid-for property Betty inherited. She assumed it was to take care of things in the one other house she inherited with no reason given to Meadow. There was no mention of the girl she was helping, and she would not reveal anything or admit to anything that was going on. She acted oblivious to it all, ending up having to live back with a husband who didn't care about her, nor she about him. A few years later, it was revealed by Betty's friend, Lucielle, that there was a young girl (Daisy) who lived down the block from Raymond's house that Betty became close to, deeply loved, and became a huge part of the girl's family. Naturally, the property was hers to do with as she wanted. But these houses could have been left to the family, a legacy that could help her great-niece and great-nephew in their life. This wasn't about their greed; it was about making financial sense in a world that can easily take things away from you.

Betty moved back in with Earl, with one of the bedrooms hers to sleep in and keep her things. They led two separate lives under one roof, coexisting as a loving husband and wife to the outside world. The room became her sanctuary, a safe place to be, all her memorabilia and clothes piled high around the bed, along with any legal papers, bank statements, and finished checkbooks all rubber banded together. These things were close by and safe. Her life was all around this space with mementos and pictures that comforted Betty, holding in her mind a life of giving to others.

35

SWITCHED ROLES

EARL PASSED AWAY A FEW years later, and Betty was left to live alone in the house. She became a bit of a recluse, laying on the couch with the tv on all day. She still drove, getting groceries and things here and there. But the signs of her mind starting to regress became more evident: a slip on the garage steps, a stove burner left on, forgetting to pay bills. Meadow would check on her with calls and stopping by. She realized it was time Aunt Betty had some help.

A trip to her doctor confirmed Betty was in the beginning stages of dementia. With the doctor writing a letter to the DMV, revoking her driving privileges, Meadow decided to hire a young lady to buy Aunt Betty's groceries, help her around the house, take her to doctor's appointments and anything else. She didn't live there but was available for any needs. In many families, someone steps up and helps with their elderly. With Meadow and Betty's history, it was smarter (and saner for Meadow) to have someone neutral be involved. Betty would have continued driving and something would have happened to her or someone else. She was adamant she could still drive, her car being right in the garage. Betty kept asking, "Why do I need a driver? I have my own car I can drive!" That prompted the sale of her car, helping her finances for the next step.

This is quite typical in these situations, the person being defiant, not wanting to have help. Betty had been independent her whole life, even when married to Earl. She finally gave in and just accepted any help given to her, even though she'd make snide remarks to Meadow about all of this. "Do you think I'm crazy, do you want to put me someplace out of the way?!" Betty would ask repeatedly. It's a situation that many are faced with, and it takes a strong will and determination to handle all this effectively, keeping finances in mind along with the welfare of the individual. Because Meadow was taught respect, she was the one that needed to make sure everything was handled correctly for Aunt Betty's last years of life. No looking back, no blaming. The niece forged ahead and got everything done for her care.

Betty finally had to live in a care facility. She was livid about this, which didn't matter because she needed constant care. There was just enough money to get her started there, but the house and belongings had to be sold to cover further expenses. Meadow had legal power of attorney, being executor of whatever estate was left. This gave her the ability to sell the house even though it wasn't in Betty's name. It was a loophole blessing that saved this lady so she could be properly cared for. Meadow organized an estate sale, and she got the house sold. Her adult son, Theo, helped with finances, with Melissa there for anything else the family needed.

The beginning facility had been a local motel changed into a care center, with each resident having their own "apartment." It had a central dining room and a living area with a TV and comfortable seating. The problem was, Betty never thought of herself as old, referring to the other residents as "*those* old ones." Mixing with them was out of the question for her. Meadow and her family decorated the room with Betty's belongings and family photos. No matter how comfortable they made it, Aunt Betty would not let herself feel at home or accept this change.

With arthritis in her hands and feet, she used a cane to walk, then eventually had to be in a wheelchair. With her mind getting worse and not being able to bathe or eat by herself, it was time to move her to another care facility that housed only three residents in another town. There were visits by Meadow and her family, conversations about different times in Betty's life she could relate to, family pictures and mementos placed around her space. After her money was running out, the family searched and found a state-run facility that Betty could live in. When you think of state-run you would assume that it is an unkept facility, residents all over the place moaning, smells that aren't inviting, and staff that move slowly to get things done. That was not the case at all. This place was a tight-run ship, with great care and constant calls about what was going on. New laws had been put in place to protect the elderly, and rightly so.

Betty lived at the state-run facility for a few years, staying in bed virtually the whole time. She was cognizant and could respond when spoken to. Meadow kept asking the caregivers to take her to the next section to get her hair styled and cut but the lady adamantly refused. The niece knew Aunt Betty would be shocked if she saw what she looked like, being so vain and beautiful for most of her life. Her hair was white, long, and straggly. When Betty was showed images of herself, she'd say, "Who's that? She is such an old lady!"

Betty's Elizabeth Taylor beauty had faded, along with her agreeable conversation she cultivated during her lifetime. Her memories only showed her what a great person she was, taking care of others, giving her time and energy to show the world she was the "good girl" in her family. Nothing came up about the negative effect she had on her niece, nor how her discipline could be construed as abuse. *Without me, Meadow would be on the street, some drunken fool just like her parents*, was Aunt Betty's continual justification in her mind. *I'm the good girl...*

36

ONE JOURNEY ENDS, ANOTHER BEGINS

WHEN BETTY FINALLY PASSED AT the age of ninety-three, Meadow thought, *This is it... I will be free of all her beatings, judgment, and bad memories.* But that just wasn't the case. Those traumatic memories would stay with her always, at times getting in the way of an otherwise happy day. The situations that Meadow was in growing up, the fierce discipline at the hands of her Aunt Betty, and the psychosis of Virginia were all mental visuals that Meadow couldn't always tuck away somewhere in her brain. The key was to see someone to share this with, revealing the true nature of her childhood.

During her aunt's final days, Meadow verbally and mentally forgave Betty, whispering the affirmation while the woman lay comatose in her hospital bed. Reaching adulthood and becoming a parent gave Meadow the insight to understand how demanding life can be, that being responsible for a child is not to be taken lightly. The logical part of her mind could rationalize that Aunt Betty felt she had to raise her niece strictly, compensating for the lack of the parents' morals. Fighting with that logic, the emotional, hurt child felt Aunt Betty had a need to have power over something in her life, a result of her childhood trauma, which had taken away that power. Meadow was the perfect opportunity to regain that power, using discipline as a mask to conquer the weakness Betty felt in her.

Meadow started to see a therapist once more time. She learned through therapy to let herself grieve now that the aunt was gone and to let everything come to the surface. She had to give herself time to heal, forgiving the parties involved, as well as herself. Meadow knew the abuse wasn't her fault. But there was always the mantra, *I'll be a better girl*, that would come up in her thoughts.

The therapist shared something that had worked for many of her patients: if you grow a mental tree by planting its seed, allowing it to grow, you can begin to heal. As each branch grows and bears fruit, that fruit (representing the memory) will fall off and fade away to somewhere else in your mind, not hidden, but kept as a reference of how your life traveled. This is painful for sure, but, with each growth spurt of the tree, those memories will stay in another place, letting you be free to live your life to the fullest. There is no age or time limit with this memory freedom. Meadow worked on this, slowly becoming more healed by the trauma that was caused from the mental and physical abuse she was exposed to.

Meadow's life has been fruitful—with grandchildren now, a solid marriage, and time to just, well, *live*. How she would have turned out living with her parents instead of her grandparents, we'll never know. She ended up being a fighter who would not give up when anything happened in her life. This quality could have turned into spiteful hate, ruining her, and blaming the world for her troubles. Drugs, alcohol, or even suicide could have easily been her way of dealing with the abuse; it would have been a life of ruin caused by her physical and emotional situation. Instead, it taught her not to give up and to keep fighting for what she believed in, forging ahead no matter what obstacles happen in her life. She strives to keep a positive attitude, a glass "half full" philosophy that makes her life follow a path of survival. Along with this mindset, Meadow was graced with the innate ability to not transfer the repeated trauma to her husband, children and grandchildren or anyone else in her life.

Aunt Betty and the memories of her abusive discipline will never be gone for Meadow. Yet the tree she carefully planted will continue to grow, bearing fruit, with each bad memory drifting off and away as the fruit falls from the tree. Although Pete and Janie didn't have the strength to thwart all of Betty's discipline, Meadow understood that turning a *blind eye* to some of the trauma was the only way that the grandparents knew how to survive the situation. She does not judge them for that, and Meadow will forever have the happy memories of being loved and cared for by Pete and Janie. It's that love she can hold onto, feeling safe when she thinks of them. The memory of her walking hand in hand with Grampa Pete and Grama Janie, wandering through the beautiful fields of alfalfa on their ranch, with the setting sun fading into the hills that caress the beautiful Pacific Ocean is what she fondly remembers…cherishing their love that continually comforts Meadow through her rich life she is so blessed to have.

EPILOGUE

FINAL MUSINGS

ONE THING THAT IS EVIDENT throughout this tale is that our family is just that: our family. They are who they are, and we cannot expect them to change. Most of us fit into a hierarchy of siblings: oldest, youngest, or somewhere in between, with some being the only child. Throughout our life we will always remain in that place in our family. I did think it would change as I got older. Being the baby of the family and years younger than my siblings, I have remained "Little Joey" and learned to be ok with that. For years I wanted to be thought of as an equal. Not that I haven't been accepted and loved for who I am, but that the *hierarchy* seems to remain the same. Once I understood and accepted this fact, I've been much happier and understanding of how families work, as well as the world. Betty and Virginia are a prime example of how siblings can cause each other pain throughout their lives…a waste of time that never solves anything and only brings pain.

Various generations experience things culturally. The expanse of knowledge is vast and a welcoming necessity for continued survival. What we need to be aware of is that we come alone, and we go alone. Searching your soul and becoming aware of who we are, admitting our faults and abilities is key for mental survival. Denying who we are will only wreak havoc in our lives. Once that is achieved and we *understand* ourselves and our culture, the journey can be mindfully fruitful. When we make a mistake, we need to own it and forge ahead. No self-flogging or doubting of who we are, being a victim because of this or that. It's a waste of time and serves no purpose. Praising ourselves for doing good things is just as important.

So, travel on, stay safe, and love yourself. I know that is difficult at times, yet it is the only way we can truly love others and accept them for who *they* are. If it takes time, it takes time. Please give yourself that time, and self-love will come and make your life the pleasure it should be. After all, that clock does tick…

ABOUT THE AUTHOR

JP Guggia has been a floral designer for most of his career, having owned a brick-and-mortar flower shop for thirty-three years. Since closing that shop in 2011, he has been a studio florist, designing daily work, weddings, and all types of floral creations.

He has written articles for floral publications and various blogs. *Blind-Eye Love* is his first foray into the book publishing world, and his true hope is to continue writing with the goal of making a difference in the world, concentrating on period novels that expand the life and outlook of his readers, giving them a true perspective to understand the human element.

Connect with the author on his social media pages:

Instagram: https://www.instagram.com/joeguggia/

Facebook: https://www.facebook.com/joe.guggia